THE BEAST OF THE HAITIAN HILLS

THE ᗷEAST OF THE ᕼAITIAN ᕼILLS

By Philippe Thoby-Marcelin
and Pierre Marcelin

translated from the French by Peter C. Rhodes

with an afterword by Philippe Thoby-Marcelin

CITY LIGHTS BOOKS
San Francisco

Cover painting by P. Pierre, courtesy, The Selden Rodman
Collection of Popular Art in Oakland, New Jersey

Library of Congress Cataloging-in-Publication Data

Thoby-Marcelin, Philippe, 1904–1975.
The beast of the Haitian hills.

Translation of: la bête du Musseau.
I. Marcelin, Pierre, 1908–   . II. Title.
PQ3949.T45B413 1986   843   86-974
ISBN 0-87286-189-9 (pbk.)

CITY LIGHTS BOOKS are edited by Lawrence Ferlinghetti
& Nancy J. Peters and published at the City Lights Bookstore,
261 Columbus Avenue, San Francisco, California 94133

"It was there for the first time that she felt that special hallucination peculiar to country people, alertly watching for the apparition of some fantastic animal, the passage of the 'Great Beast' which nearly all of her small companions had seen at least once. . . . This element of the fantastic appeared to her to be one of the strongest influences in people's thinking. She noticed it particularly among those poor people who seemed unable, except by the play of their bold imaginations, to react against the rude misery of their material lives."

Emile Caro: *George Sand*

MORIN DUTILLEUL: city grocer who becomes a planter at Musseau
EUGENIE: his wife
BOSSUET METELUS: influential peasant in league with evil spirits
DESILUS: Morin's hired man
SOR CIE: Bossuet's wife
TI-CHARLES: Bossuet's younger brother
DELISCA DELICE: Chief Constable of the region around Musseau
MADAN HORACE: the shopkeeper, Bossuet's sister and Horace's wife
HORACE: a carpenter
CHERISENA: Madan Horace's goddaughter
SINETTE: Morin's maidservant
IRMA: Ti-Charles' fiancee
HOUNGAN ROSSINI: a voodoo priest
THE CIGOUAVE: "the thing," an evil spirit
ALCAEUS: Irma's father
POLYCARP: Delice's adjutant
BARON SAMEDI: Voodoo God of Death
SOR TI-MA: midwife of Musseau
VIERGINE: Desilus' godmother
YVONNE REGIS: Eugenie Dutilleul's friend
OGOUN BADAGRIS: Desilus' guardian spirit

orin Dutilleul, a grocer by trade, had always dreamed of becoming a planter. It had been his earliest ambition. When he was a little boy, his parents took him to Bourdon during the hot months and since that first taste of country life he had always wanted to return. Although he grew up in the city, he nurtured his romantic taste for rural life by reading idealized accounts of it. In fact, he had no understanding of life in the hills. The painful and savage struggle of the small mountain share-cropper with the elements was a closed book to him.

To Morin Dutilleul country life was, above all, the luscious mango season. It was the season of tumultuous children in the swimming holes of the mountain torrents of the Wood-of-Oaks; the season of the songs of the black washerwomen, with skirts lifted above strong bare thighs as they beat their clothes upon the stream's stony banks; the season of enchanting tales and guessing games drawn from the mysterious night, when the thick foliage of the trees took on the shapes of phantoms and all the other exciting scenes of his youth which time had etched upon his mind.

And of course he faintly remembered that the torrent in the ravine, swollen by sudden summer cloudbursts, would sometimes go wild with fury. It would carry away whole portions of the mountainside and toss huge trees as though they were matchwood and carry off men and animals to the sea. But such scenes now were like faraway poetry in his mind.

Besides, his comfortable life as a shopkeeper seemed drab

to him. Being a mulatto descendant of the former colonial caste of freedmen, he believed in the "back to the land" dogma, that everlasting slogan of the country's economists who want to be credited with realistic common sense. As for Morin Dutilleul, however, it was anything but a pretense or a political springboard. He had it, so to speak, in his blood. His ancestors, like all Haitians of their class, had been planters, and as he recalled this nostalgically, he considered his present position a loss of status.

The only obstacle to making his dream real was his wife, a little woman with a guileless face and slanting Chinese eyes. She had lovely curling hair and the smooth bronzed skin of a Sulamite. From the moment that the exquisite charms of his sweet Eugenie conquered him, he understood that it would be impossible to transplant this fragile being to the harsh and isolated life of a plantation in the hills. And so he had bowed to the will of fate.

For six years he loved Eugenie with a tender passion, in which the flesh, alas, played but a slight part. He was, however, a man of the tropics, whose passions were easily aroused but rarely appeased. Although his sentimental ardor was cooled daily, he became resentful towards his wife for this indulgence which had made him dependent upon her for so long. Her love was too tender. In fact, she alone stood in the way of his desire to become a landowner. And he increasingly longed for more elemental and stronger physical pleasures.

This led him to seek the charms of other women. Having little time to play fast and loose, he chose as his associates the blackest among the women who came to his store, dragging them excitedly into the small back room. There he had only to close his eyes to find again in a flash the lovely valley of Bourdon and the glistening thighs of the singing washer-women of his childhood days.

Then he began to neglect Eugenie, who was amazed at the change in her husband. She had grown accustomed to be importuned by him each night for some coarse pleasure which she rarely shared, and which always left her with an infinite sadness and a crushing weight of fatigue. But she was not a suspicious woman and as he returned home regularly at the same time, she had not the slightest idea of his unfaithfulness. It is true that as a child in the Saint Rose of Lima convent school she had always been the most devout member of her class.

At last she talked to a friend who advised her to have a child and sent her to an old doctor who was reputed to know how to cure the most stubborn cases of sterility. She followed his treatment without telling her husband and soon she was happy to feel the first signs of pregnancy.

But when Morin heard the news, far from feeling the proud thrill of a father, he was seized with a sudden fore-boding, for he had always feared the risks of childbirth for his young and delicate wife. All the tenderness which he had buried deep within himself, and which had appeared exhausted, suddenly rose to his lips.

"My God, what a situation!" he whispered in a broken voice, holding his head in his hands. "I would never have believed this possible. . . ."

So he didn't want a baby! Eugenie thought, hiding her emotion behind a faint smile. She felt as if someone had pulled a high ladder from under her. She struggled to keep from fainting.

"So . . . you are not pleased by the news?"

He looked up at her. That expression of a trapped ani-

animal, those trembling lips! Suddenly, guessing the pain he was inflicting on her, Morin tried to make up for the shock of his surprise.

"What are you saying? Look at me, Eugenie . . . You're not going to think that I . . ."

He took her hands in his big fists—her little hands!—drew her to him and kissed her as one might kiss a child that one has just thrashed.

"It's just that I wasn't expecting it," he murmured.

Morin's worst fears were confirmed. At seven months Eugenie gave birth to a tiny baby boy, skinny and wrinkled, who lived only a few minutes. There was not even time to baptize him. She, however, seemed to have pulled through safely. The doctor had cleaned up and gone, leaving her asleep. Morin was in the living room with the neighbors who had gathered at the news. Suddenly Eugenie awoke, startled, her eyes filled with fear, and motioned to the midwife to lift the covers.

"Quick, see what's wrong with me," she whispered, leaning forward on her elbows. "I feel soaking wet."

A treacherous hemorrhage had struck her while she slept. Already she lay in the midst of a great red stain.

"Blood!" she murmured, letting her head fall back on the pillows. "Just what I thought."

Morin, informed, ran to the telephone to call back the doctor. Relatives and friends scurried about trying to help; but all their efforts proved in vain. By the time the doctor arrived, it was already too late. Eugenie could no longer see, so weak had she become from loss of blood. The midwife, holding her pulse, made a discouraged gesture. Morin pushed her aside with firmness and bent down towards Eugenie, trembling.

"It's me . . . your husband . . . Can you hear me?"

The scarecrow of a man broke down, voicing the most absurd hopes. His throat filled with tears, cracked into whining monologue.

"Eugenie . . . You are all I have in the world . . . You can't leave me alone like this . . ."

She already showed the signs of approaching death, but somehow she found the strength to smile. Her lips twitched and he thought he heard her speak.

"I loved you . . . so very much . . . you know."

They buried her the next day.

It had rained during the night, and as the procession entered the cemetery the warm and luscious odor of the earth, in a cruel association of ideas, brought back to Morin's mind all the infidelities he had committed. Even yesterday, only a few hours before the accident . . . His shame was so strong that he raised his hand to his eyes and stumbled. His friends, thinking he was about to faint, tried to support him. He withdrew from their arms with a gesture of impatience.

What hypocrisy that would be! he thought.

And everyone near him was surprised to hear him murmur to himself:

"My God, how could I let myself do such filthy things!"

Not knowing of what he was talking, they believed he had for a moment become delirious.

When the last friends left the house after the funeral, Morin Dutilleul felt relieved. The crowded excitement which surrounds a death or a funeral had, it is true, somewhat dulled his sorrow; but secretly there remained deep inside him, like a hard fruit stone, the atrocious sensation of an irreparable calamity. It marked its presence by sharp and knifelike pains. Then he gave way to his violent sorrow and opened all the outlets to this burning lava, compressed within the depths of his flesh. He went to his room, and threw himself sobbing upon his bed.

He cried for a long time. Then all was quiet.

When he awakened it was already night. All the faces of those who had sought his caresses crowded about him.

"Courage, Dutilleul!" they murmured.

There could be no doubt. Eugenie was dead. It was certainly true. He had not been dreaming.

He switched on the light and beside him on his bedside table he saw the large glass of milk which the maid usually brought him before going to bed. He swallowed it in one gulp. Now everything about him was calm. The east wind, pouring down from the nearby mountains, softly pushed the venetian blinds and penetrated the room. He was no longer in revolt against this dreadful reality. But he was completely overwhelmed by it.

Although he was a healthy and vigorous man in the prime of life, Morin Dutilleul let himself be consumed with regret longer than the average widower. He was implacably pursued by the thought that never again would he see his wife, and obsessed by the memory of his amorous adventures in the back room of his grocery store.

Now that he was free again and nothing more stood in the way of his going to live in the country, he created in himself a superstitious horror of this persistent fancy, obscurely fearing that it might have been the sinister cause of Eugenie's death. He tried to suppress this odious accusation which was only half-formed and confused inside him. But it obstinately returned to the fringes of his conscience.

Finally, hoping that he might find oblivion by fleeing from a setting which in every detail recalled the past, he sold his shop, rented his house and moved to a room in a hotel. But that was even worse. Both idleness and the complete inactivity of his mind deprived him of any refuge from his sorrow.

Soon he gave himself up to drink. It was a form of punishment he enjoyed inflicting on himself, to vary his suffering, and also a way of seeking to destroy himself. Men in despair always flee from their torment to alcohol and drugs, or religion or women or suicide. He made his own choice. Could anyone reproach him for it?

Bit by bit he degraded himself. He frequented the most sordid and ignoble places, sinking down a step lower each day, and finding a certain relief in swallowing his pride and in humiliating himself. That was the perversity of the Christian in him. And yet Morin Dutilleul, since the mystical flights of his chaste but troubled adolescence, had lost all faith.

Never, in his most degenerate orgies, did he approach women. It was not that his flesh was drugged by his excessive drinking bouts. On the contrary, his eroticism was whipped to even greater intensity by them. Only remorse kept him from giving way to his natural impulses.

One morning when Joyous, the hotel chambermaid, brought his coffee to his room, he was troubled to see her stand in such a queer way that her belly protruded lewdly, a coarse temptation close to him. She was a girl from the hills, built to his taste, black, big thighed, robust. Her body gave off a powerful rustic odor. She had always been accommodating to the boarders, and Morin knew it. He paid her a compliment on the sprightliness of her carriage. She timidly lowered her eyes.

"Oh my, Sir! What were those naughty words you said?"

So he pulled her into bed with him. She smiled, her breasts heaved, and she did not resist his advances. When he touched her she immediately uttered sharp cries of surprise and delight:

"Ho-ho! . . . Ho-ho! . . . Ho-ho!"

He soon pushed her away from him, disgusted, thinking of Eugenie.

After that he never tried to make love again. Potent concoctions made of absinthe, anise and lemon which he drank steadily ruined his digestion. Every day he lived in agonized pain, but his remorse found new strength and became exalted. At first he wanted to give up drinking. And yet, despite the pledges he made to himself, at the end of one week of heroic temperance he voluptuously gave in to the subtle appeals of his vice, for he had let himself be dominated by it. He went so far as to seek the trances that it brought him and even learned systematically how to cultivate them. He was punishing himself. At least, that was the pretext he gave himself.

One evening as he was about to fall asleep he heard his dead wife whisper in his ear.

"Morin!"

Frightened, he sat up in bed. He knew very well that it was only a delusion of his intoxicated brain. But his fear was so great that he had to light the lamp to regain his composure. That night he was unable to close his eyes. The voice of Eugenie kept calling him.

"Morin! . . . Morin!"

The tone of her voice was anguished. It was the call of a person in distress, and it frightened Dutilleul. Again he saw his dying Eugenie; but far from smiling as she had done in her death agony, she was weeping and begging him to save her, to hold her among the living. At dawn, exhausted, he at last fell into so profound a sleep that it seemed like the darkness of eternity.

Two weeks passed before the hallucination was repeated. From then on they came more and more frequently, and he ended by enjoying them, as he had his agonizing cramps. Finally, he could summon up his wife's ghost simply by drinking a glass of milk as he went to bed. And now his dead spouse was no longer content to call him, she would also speak with him.

"Morin!" she said to him once. "You are the one who killed me!"

As he protested his innocence, Eugenie insisted, and defined her accusation more precisely.

"You wanted me to die, I know it," she said. "You wanted to live in the country, and for that it was necessary that I should go away. So I left, for I loved you more than myself."

Morin broke down and sobbed.

"It's true, Eugenie! It's true! . . . But look how unhappy I am now. Forgive me. . . ."

"And why should I forgive you, my friend? I don't hold it against you. Where I am nobody suffers, and none can hurt you. No one. Do you hear, Morin? No one!"

Another time, she spoke to him of his infidelities, but

without the slightest reproach. She even justified them, going so far as to tell him that it was her fault for not having known how to satisfy him.

And thus it was that Morin Dutilleul was able, little by little, to ease his conscience. It was a strange comedy he played upon himself, with the complicity of his viscera. Only by this exquisite intimacy with his dead wife was he able to free himself from all his scruples, as some faithful souls do through confession.

In the end, when all his torments of conscience had been cleared, she asked him to drink no more.

"Why don't you go and settle down in the country, as you always wanted to do in the past?" she asked him one night. "Perhaps there, by working hard and by exercising a little will power, you can rid yourself of your vice."

"That's a good idea," he eagerly agreed. "You are right, Eugenie. I will try."

t was an afternoon late in March, when the weather still hesitated between winter drought and the spring rains. The sun had just set softly behind the green slopes of the ridge which skirted the western edge of the country hamlet of Musseau. The air was clear, and the sun had gone down without its usual explosive red glow. The sky remained suffused with its light, filtered down to earth from the high atmosphere, as evening lingered on. The thin white moon rose in the sky and the air grew chill, its faint breath fluttering the delicate leaves of the bayahonda trees.

Morin Dutilleul was still taking his siesta in a hammock slung between the branches of a giant mango tree. Nearby on a table stood a decanter of rum and an earthen pitcher of water covered with a glass. A swarm of tiny tropical flies, attracted by the abundant saliva, darkened the corners of his lips. His arm rose rhythmically, instinctively driving off the flies, but they constantly returned when his arm dropped. Finally the torment of their repeated attacks awakened him. He rubbed his eyes, looked blankly about him and finally recognized the estate that he had just bought. He broke into a satisfied smile, filled with youthful pride.

He had, in fact, struck a good bargain; about ten squares of land bought for a song, with a house thrown in and, at the foot of a hill, an abundant little spring whose flow disappeared under the pebbles of a dry mountain stream-bed, after running a few yards over a bed of fine, clean sand. Of course the house was old and its beams were worm-eaten, but it would stand for some years longer. He planned in any case to rebuild it as soon as possible, so that it would be worthy of a modern and progressive planter. Until that day he would sleep in the garret, whose windows he left open to the four winds. On the ground floor three spacious rooms were surrounded by a roofed gallery paved with red tiles.

That evening Morin Dutilleul smiled, something that rarely happened since his wife's death. But his pleasure was fleeting. A confused hubbub from the direction of the spring assailed his ears.

"That dirty riffraff again!" he groaned.

His mouth twisted in an angry sneer. He was no longer the Morin of former days, the idealistic town dweller poetically dreaming from afar of the beauties of rural life. Since he had come into contact with the peasants, he now found them on close inspection too uncouth and poverty-stricken and, despite this, "without the slightest respect for well-to-do folk." And so, hardly had he settled down at Musseau than Morin set himself the task of demanding respect for himself by adopting a distant, almost arrogant, attitude towards them; which perhaps was not, after all, unwise, for, although their ancestors had abolished colonial slavery at the price of their blood, these poor people were still held down by the ruling class in chains of servitude, ignorance and misery. While they still found duties imposed upon them, they hardly were aware that they also had rights, and everything was done so that they remained in that benign state of ignorance. But resigned as they seemed, it would not be good to let them believe that they could be, when the occasion presented itself, the stronger or the smarter.

Morin Dutilleul, who had proven so adept at his trade of grocer, made one blunder after another as a planter at Musseau. And yet he had not been drunk for some time now, except for an occasional Sunday, when despair would creep back upon him under cover of his enforced inactivity. His attitude was marked by the bitterness that great disillusionment sometimes brings. He suffered because the reality of peasant life revealed itself so different from his idyllic dream of the past. So, passing from one extreme to the other, he soon found himself detesting the farmers. Once in a while, recalling his dead wife, he was seized by a profound disgust of himself.

"That I should have fallen so low, truly . . ." he would muse.

More than ever now he believed in the goodness of the land. And yet the country folk who lived around him seemed so utterly odious, stupid and filthy that all the waters of the sea would not suffice to cleanse them. He even deplored their presence in the countryside, though he knew perfectly well that it belonged more to them than to him and his class. They constituted an insurmountable obstacle to progress on the land, he illogically said to himself.

"No," groaned Morin as the bickering suddenly rose to the scandalous proportions of an uproar. "No, I cannot allow things to continue like this!"

He leaped from the hammock and walked briskly towards the spring with long, nervous steps. There he found three little Negro girls, clothed in filthy rags, quarreling and shouting at each other for the sheer pleasure of it, simply training themselves in the useful and popular art of invective. At the sight of Morin, whose fury was apparent, they ceased their game and burst out laughing.

"Little pests!" he shouted as they skipped lightly across the stream-bed. "Just let me catch you here once more and you'll see what you'll get from me! This is the last warning I'll give you!"

"Huh!" the boldest of them insolently shouted back, her fists akimbo, wriggling her torso in disdain despite the large sun-baked calabash she balanced perfectly on her head. "Do you even realize what you're saying to us now? You're soused! . . . No, my friends, no! Just take a look at the big stiff for me!"

Morin turned white under the sting of the insult. So they were aware of his vice! He bent down to pick up some stones to throw at them when a man appeared from the bushes on the opposite bank.

"I see," the newcomer sharply scolded, "you young scamps have no respect for your elders. How dare you insult this gentleman? Master Morin lets you draw water from his spring and that's the way you thank him? Very well, we'll see what you'll get for that! I'm going to tell your parents so they'll skin you alive with the whip. And you can sprinkle soot on your behinds after that to ease the pain, for all I care."

After the girls had run off, holding their calabashes high, the man scrambled down the slope of the ravine and slowly climbed the mound where Morin Dutilleul stood. He was dressed in plain white drill, like a town dweller, but wore the open-backed slippers of a peasant, and a large straw palm hat ornamented with a red ribbon.

"Master," he said modestly. "I'm your neighbor, yes, sir!"

"Oh, so it's you . . . Bossuet Metelus. That is your name, isn't it?"

"Positively, Master Morin. So somebody's already spoken to you of me, since you know my name?"

"Aren't you the man who commands everyone around here?" Dutilleul answered him, smiling maliciously, a faint gleam of defiance in his eyes.

"Me, Master? What a foolish idea! Surely someone who doesn't like me has told you such a silly story. But you shouldn't listen to people like that, for they're only spiteful. And then you know very well that big words only kill little dogs, don't you?"

The adage pleased Morin, not only because of the humorous flavor with which it was said, but also for the wisdom that it seemed to denote in the man who had been described to him in the most unfavorable light, as a hothead and even as a loafer.

"As for me, Master," Bossuet Metelus hypocritically continued, "I am only a poor toiler of the land, and I have never tried to hang my kit-bag higher than my arms can reach."

Amused, almost taken in (he certainly seemed one of the ideal peasants that Morin had once dreamed them to be), Morin patted him familiarly on the shoulder and invited him up for a glass of rum. Bossuet Metelus did not hesitate to accept. He had expected this friendly offer. Between neighbors who know the customs of the countryside, he thought, isn't courtesy to be expected, whatever the respective wealth and social position of the men? But in this he too fed himself with illusions, for to Morin Dutilleul the invitation was nothing more than a favor.

As they reached the mango tree Bossuet Metelus ran his eyes over the property, turning slowly, as if he had never seen it before.

"Master," he said politely. "This is certainly a good piece of land you have here. Yes, sir!"

Morin Dutilleul puffed up with pride.

"Yes, and I'm going to plant it with small millet. What do you think of that?"

"As for that, Master, there's no doubt of it. It's a good idea, yes indeed! Only if I were in your shoes, I'd also plant manioc, corn and congo peas, for it isn't wise, don't you think, to put all your chances on a single crop. When one of them doesn't fetch a good price on the market, you can make it up on the others."

"I wouldn't contradict you, neighbor Bossuet. But I'm determined to do things in a big way, and I even count on going in for pure speculation with my crops, for merchandising is my trade and I assure you I know it well."

The hired man, at Morin's order, brought an extra glass and two chairs. He greeted Bossuet Metelus with a degree of respect that neither age nor social standing seemed to warrant, and this fact did not escape the vigilant, suspicious eye of his master.

"Good evening, Desilus," Bossuet answered. "So you're the man who's working here for Master Morin?"

"Yes, it's me. . . . You see, I didn't have time to come and tell you the news myself. And then I also heard that you were in town for a fortnight or two."

"How is my godson?"

Desilus looked gloomy.

"Your godson is well. Yes, godfather Bossuet. He's even too well. If you only knew how much he resembles me at the present time! One would think this child had come to take my place on earth. The more he grows, the more I feel my own strength ebbing away from me. If this curse continues, one fine morning I'm going to wake up and find that I'm not worth more than a burnt-out candle which has gutted itself. . . ."

"Neighbor, here's to your health!" Dutilleul sharply toasted his guest. This family conversation, replete with superstition, seemed out of place, held without the slightest restraint in the presence of a stranger like himself.

"And here's to your own, Master Morin!"

Bossuet Metelus swallowed the rum in one gulp then, after clicking his tongue politely, he mused a moment.

"That must be Barbancourt Three-Star," he said, trying to show that he was a connoisseur of good things, even though he was a farmer.

And Morin finally understood that, despite the modest air he put on, this peasant intended to deal with him on an equal footing, and the realization did not fail to irritate him. He thought it was time to show this man his ill humor.

"Neighbor!" he resumed brusquely, "as I told you a little while ago, I'm going to build up a large plantation. But I'm told there are thieves around here. Let those who set foot on my land beware! I know how to deal with them."

Bossuet Metelus smiled with a deliberately innocent air and scratched the back of his neck carelessly.

"Master, yes, there are thieves around here. They rob me, they rob the other villagers, but they'll never dare to come near your place. You know the old saying: the pig knows against which tree he can scratch himself."

"What's more, I'm taking no chances," Morin continued. "I'm going to fence in my property. I've already bought the barbed wire. If, in spite of that, any bold person tries to step on my land, I'll shoot him straight in the heart with my pistol, and he'll deserve what he gets."

"Master Morin, once you've fenced the plantation, who would dare to enter upon your property to rob you?"

"I don't know who it might be. But I ask you to warn all the people around here of what I've said. I know them well already. They have a way of showing their fine teeth in a friendly smile when you're looking their way, and then giving you a couple of swift kicks when your back is turned. When you're nice to them they take it for a sign of weakness, and hasten to abuse you. Look at the spring! I'm going to fence it in too. What else can I do? I allow them to draw their water; instead they use it for their noisy bickering and prevent me from taking a quiet nap on my own property. I've been insulted. Very well! They'll soon learn what manner of a man I really am!"

The glowing spring twilight had lingered for a long time, but now night crept up on padded feet and the moon flooded the countryside with her thick golden honey. As the servant began to light the lamps in the house, Bossuet rose to say good-bye.

"Master, I must take my leave now. It is late."

The neutral tone of his voice revealed his hurt pride.

Morin understood that he had made a blunder and tried to ease its effects.

"Oh, ho, what's hurrying you, neighbor?" he said, trying to appear cordial. "Won't you have a last grog for the road?"

Bossuet could not refuse, but he accepted the drink with marked coolness.

The next morning Morin Dutilleul began planting. He had chosen the land around spring to transplant banana sprouts, as the damp soil would make them mature quickly and develop heavy bunches. Stripped to the waist, his pants rolled above his knees, Desilus was drilling holes with a long crowbar. Each time he drove it into the moist, soft earth a loud groan escaped from his lips, as if the effort tore at his lungs. To see the old man was truly enough to make one believe, as he claimed, that his son sapped his father's strength as he grew up.

While Desilus worked Morin stood about, supervising his efforts with a severe eye and giving him plenty of free advice.

"The holes must be deep," he would say. "If not, the first strong wind will blow the banana trees to the ground."

"Yes, sir, Mist' Dutilleul."

"Desilus, you should be careful not to plant the shoots too close to each other. Otherwise they won't get enough nourishment to grow well."

"Yes, sir, Mist' Dutilleul."

This had been going on since early morning. Finally tired of all this free advice, which he, one of the most expert of farmers, deeply resented, Desilus could hold his tongue no longer.

"You needn't worry, Mist' Dutilleul," he muttered. "As for farm work, I know all about it. Why, I was still a tiny boy running around in a ragged shrift, my navel open to every breeze, when my father first took me with him to help him plant banana sprouts. I've done more farm work than you could shake a stick at."

Morin grew angry in turn.

"Now there's the smart-aleck attitude that I don't like in you! All you ignorant Haitian Negroes are the same," he exploded. "You certainly have nerve! You always pretend you already know anything anyone ever tries to show you, better than they do. Now, get a move on! You know nothing, absolutely nothing about anything, do you understand?"

"I don't know about many other things," Desilus humbly retorted, profoundly annoyed. "No, Mist' Dutilleul, I admit I don't know about many things. Which is more than you're willing to admit honestly to yourself. But as to what is called the business of farming, I can assure you I know it well. My entire family lived on the land. What's more, they always managed to raise enough to eat, and for their other modest needs. And as for the man you see standing here before you, my mother's milk still left its dew on my upper lip when I learned how to wield a hoe!"

Just at that moment Bossuet showed up, stepping out from behind a thicket of guava bushes on the opposite side of the ravine.

"Good morning, Master Morin," he called smoothly.

He remained on the other bank, obsequiously holding his hat in his hand.

"I see, Master, that you're planting banana trees. It's the right season for that, yes indeed. The rains will soon be here and then they'll get off to a fine start."

He smiled slyly, and seemed to be laughing aloud to

himself. Morin felt like sending him out to pasture once and for all. But Bossuet, who divined his feelings only too well, didn't let himself be disarmed by this hostility. He even pushed his daring further.

"Master Morin, I don't know if it would bother you in the midst of all your work, but I would like to show you over my plantation sometime."

Whatever caused this show of self-assurance—for the invitation manifestly was in the nature of a challenge—Morin accepted his offer. He was determined to assert his superiority over this country bumpkin. He felt a bitter rivalry springing up between the two of them, and the time had come to make this rustic understand that he did not fear him in the slightest degree.

They entered the thick jungle undergrowth, moving along a narrow path carpeted with rotting vegetation and leaves. The acrid odor of vegetable decay, hot and humid, literally dripped from the thick foliage all about them. Bossuet walked in front, armed with a machete, with which he hacked away the thorny branches thrusting across their path. Morin followed several paces behind out of reach of the flashing blade, listening to the melancholy cooing of doves in the thickets and to the barely perceptible murmur of young plants patiently pushing their way upward, seeking sunlight. Soon they broke out of the jungle on the edge of a field planted with millet, which was maturing its second and last growth after a first cutting. Morin was really amazed at the breadth of the planted field.

"All this belongs to you?" he asked.

A thin smile of satisfaction crossed Bossuet Metelus's

face. Yes, but that wasn't the only one of his cultivated fields. No, this was only the area planted under millet which the Master looked upon, he explained. He thought this would convince Morin of the excellence of his work. But he was wrong. Morin had something more to say.

"Neighbor," he said ponderously. "You are a hard-working man, as I can see, and I compliment you for it. But it's really a shame that you don't know the science of cultivation."

"What's that?" Bossuet exclaimed, his eyes wide with astonishment. "You mean me, Master? You think I don't know how to farm?"

"That's right, neighbor, you do not know."

"Ho-ho! Ho-ho! Well, just listen to the Master speak!"

"To show you exactly what I mean, I will only point out to you, neighbor, that it's not smart to force two crops from millet. After the first crop you should immediately strip out the plants by the roots, plow the land again and plant some other seed. Otherwise your second crop will be too thin. But then, of course, you small farmers can subsist on very little. As for me, I expect more out of life."

Bossuet Metelus stroked his chin thoughtfully, holding himself in to keep from laughing right in the face of this city slicker whose artlessness was glaring and who thought he could teach him, Bossuet, how to farm.

"Soon, neighbor," Morin gravely continued, "I will begin my planting in earnest. And then one of these days you'll see if what I've told you isn't right."

"Oh, Master Morin, I never doubted it! I know already that you are right. Since you have assured me that it is so, I believe you."

Then they visited other cultivated fields, fields planted

with manioc, sweet potatoes, congo peas, ground squash, and on each occasion Morin would proffer some criticism. This amused the farmer very much, although he pretended every time to agree with everything Morin told him.

Finally, after looking over each of the fields, they sauntered up to the peasant's cabin. There were three people under the arbor in front of the house: Sor Cie, Bossuet's wife, also known among the villagers as Madan Bossuet, who was chatting with the chief constable of the region, and Ti-Charles, Bossuet's youngest brother, who was seated not far from them on an upturned wooden mortar for grinding corn, listening idly to their gossip. Ti-Charles was handsome by Negro esthetic standards, for he had small, delicate ears. He was a dashing young man in his early twenties, did not take the advice of his elders seriously, and had turned the hearts of all the young women of the region.

Bossuet introduced Morin to each of them. The newcomer immediately turned to the police chief, whose social standing in any small Haitian hill community is great. Appointed by the central government, the rural police chiefs are empowered with complete authority for the maintenance of order in the communities over which they preside.

"I am indeed glad to meet you here," Morin said to him. "I have something very important to discuss with you."

He told him of reports he had heard about the robbers who infested the region of Musseau and of his decision to fence his property and the spring. He raised his voice to the tone of command. Disagreeably impressed, those present looked blandly at him, nodding their heads vigorously.

They understood that Master Dutilleul did not intend to be a friendly neighbor and that he would never miss any opportunity of causing them trouble. When Morin had finished, the chief constable answered him calmly.

"As for disorder, Master, I can assure you that we don't know of any hereabouts. Once you've fenced in your land I can guarantee that neither beast nor man will trespass on your estate. I, Delisca Delice, justice of the peace under his own command, affirm that before you all. And you can believe what I say, Master."

But his assurances were not enough for Morin.

"Ask Bossuet what happened yesterday at the spring," he said.

The chief constable looked at Bossuet with consternation.

"Yes indeed, Constable," Bossuet confirmed. "And it was my own sister's adopted goddaughters who caused all the scandal. Master Morin tried to bring them to order, and they made stupid remarks in reply to him. I'm going to inform Madan Horace so that she can break every bone in their bodies."

The chief constable, who could hardly believe his ears, clicked his tongue in dismay. Sor Cie was shocked by what she heard.

"My friends, oh, dear me!" she groaned. "What can all this mean? Where have our children learned such licentiousness? What is the world coming to? One of these days, if our children continue to show such disrespect for their elders, we'll see them climb on our backs and beat us like ordinary beasts of burden!"

"If anyone needs water from the spring," Delisca Delice

concluded, "why, all they have to do is go take it. What need is there for creating a disturbance? Now see what this leads to! Master Morin is going to fence in the spring and you'll all be obliged to go far afield, perhaps as far as the fountain of Bourdon, to fill your water jugs!"

s soon as Morin had gone, the justice of the peace hurried off to Madan Horace's house. He halted politely at the foot of the steps leading to her shop and called out to her. A big woman, Madan Horace was dozing behind the counter, her head resting on her enormous breasts. She awoke with a start, squinted through her sleep-laden eyes, scratched herself energetically to recover her bearings and then sat up.

"How are you, Constable Delice?" she asked between two unstifled yawns. "And how is your family today?"

"Everyone's fine! Yes ma'am, Madan Horace," he answered politely. "And how are things with you?"

"No worse than could be expected. No."

"Has Horace gone out?"

"Yes, Sheriff, he went to the vicarage at Petionville to do a little work for Father Eusebius. You know, he is just like Father Eusebius' own son. . . ."

Madan Horace was proud of the affection the old priest showed for her husband. Horace had been brought up by the priest, who had taught him how to read, write and cipher, and as she thought this sign of partiality assured them of public esteem, she loved to boast of it on the slightest pretext.

They had, moreover, other titles to the esteem of the natives, for thanks to their general store and to her husband's skill as a carpenter, they did not live by toiling on the land. Their house, a three-room shack, roofed with tin sheet metal, was also located on the only highroad through the hamlet. Furthermore, they were married, they had three little adopted girls in their service and Horace was first tenor in the church choir.

When they went to attend high mass on Sundays at Petionville, the carpenter carried a large missal under his arm. On that holy day his wife always limped painfully in her tight holiday shoes, and would also imprison her opulent form in a long dress of black lace. They would hold hands, and as she did not know how to read, she would piously roll a rosary of glass beads that had been blessed through the fingers of her free hand, leaving the cross of gilded copper hanging elegantly at her side for all to see.

The general store displayed a wide assortment of goods. Bottles of trempes—a local concoction made of anise, absinthe and lemon juice—and kitchen oil, a pitcher of water, a basket of avocados or oranges or bananas, depending on the season, stood on the counter. Sticks of sugar cane were piled in a corner, and the shelves were loaded with little sacks of ground corn, starch, rice and unrefined red sugar. In addition, the store sold kerosene, dried codfish, red herring, salt pork, leaf tobacco, cigars, dried tripe —in short, all the merchandise required to meet the needs of the peasants of Musseau.

"Madan Horace," said the Sheriff, just as Ti-Charles came up to the store, "your adopted goddaughters yesterday afternoon went to the spring and hurled insults at Master Morin. Bossuet was there, and he can give you all the details of the incident."

The shopkeeper jumped as if she had been slapped.

"What's that you said, Constable?"

"That's right," added Ti-Charles, sitting down on the steps, "Master Morin is mad as a conger. He just announced to us that he is going to fence in the spring. Now you tell me where we are going to manage to find water, unless we go as far as the fountain of Bourdon to fetch it. That's what the reckless tricks of your miserable goddaughters have led to!"

Without wasting time to quibble about the nature of the offense, Madan Horace called the guilty girls and ordered them down on their knees before her.

"Band of vermin!" she bellowed. "Haven't you tired yet of making trouble for me?"

"It wasn't me," one of the girls protested. "It was Cherisena who told Master Morin that he was drunk."

Madan Horace heaved a great sigh.

"I was sure of it! She's always the one who drags the others into these adventures."

She had no sooner spoken than she grabbed a large wooden spoon and began to administer a severe thrashing to the girl. Cherisena writhed under the blows, screamed, begged for forgiveness, but the shopkeeper was deaf to all her pleas. She beat her unmercifully with all her strength, beat her, beat her, shouting in cadence with her flailing arm:

"You'll be quiet one day. . . . You'll stay quiet. . . . You'll stay. . . . You'll stay. . . ."

Finally the handle broke. Only then did Madan Horace cease her frantic beating, letting off her hysterical anger in copious oaths suitable for the occasion.

"These children will be the death of me one of these

days," she groaned, in a despairing tone, holding her temples and dramatically turning her eyes upward.

"Madan Horace," said the chief constable, "You've done well. Don't listen to these brazen little scamps. Your blood will turn bad if you're not careful. Yes, and you'll kill the tiny babe you bear in your womb. . . ."

Ti-Charles scowled and lit his pipe.

"It's true," he said, "that my sister's adopted goddaughters did wrong. But I still don't see why that should be a sufficient reason for Master Morin to forbid us to go near the spring of Musseau to fetch water. He certainly is doing his best to harm his neighbors. He is just being a bully. That's his own affair. But one of these days he'll learn how much it can cost to scorn his neighbors. The iron gate of the customs barrier was reputed to be tough too, but the urine of passing tramps soon split it wide open with rust."

"When a man is angry, what does he not say?" remarked Delisca Delice philosophically. "Master Morin has announced that he will close off the spring, but he hasn't done it yet. Wait a little until he calms down, and you'll see if things don't turn out alright."

"No, Constable, he'll do exactly as he has promised to do. I'm sure of it. Moreover, he began by telling us there were thieves in Musseau. And who do you think he meant? Why, it's clear he meant me, he meant Bossuet, he meant Horace. And he will not hesitate from accusing you too, one of these days, even though you are the justice of the peace."

The shopkeeper decided it was time for her to intervene in the discussion.

"Little brother," she said in a sweet, conciliatory voice,

"there's no reason for you to talk that way. As justice of the peace Delice, who is a man of great experience, thanks be to God, has just told you, Master Morin was in a rage today, but he hasn't done anything about it yet."

"He hasn't done anything yet! That's a good one! He shows us his scorn, he insults us, and you say that he hasn't done anything wrong yet!"

The justice of the peace was visibly upset by the young man's stubbornness. He took off his helmet, scratched his head, then put it on again and adjusted it carefully.

"Ti-Charles," he said with all the authority he could command. "I'm old enough to be your father. I have two sons your age. Listen well to me. I have held this position of authority for the past ten years. I know the law well, I believe. If I didn't know it, I would not have been left in my post. And I know how to get on with people. . . . Good. Now Madan Horace here is an honest person. We are also good friends. One evening, such as this one, I hear screams as I walk along. I inquire what's wrong. They tell me there's a row going on in Madan Horace's house. There, shouldn't I rush to her aid? But the law is the law. As the proverb puts it: 'When a woman does her duty as a wife, she no longer has friends'."

"Yes, and that, that's the law," the shopkeeper vigorously assented.

Delisca continued.

"Master Morin is a rich man. We others, we are poor people. He buys his piece of land, he builds a fence around it, he declares that the poor people must not trespass on his property. Very well, then the poor people must not trespass. Good. Now suppose that one day, just like that,

Master Morin should call me and say: 'Constable!' I answer him: 'What can I do for you, Master?' He says to me, 'You know Charles, he trespassed on my plantation.' Now then, am I not obliged to arrest you? Am I not obliged to drag you off to town and throw you into prison in Fort Sunday?"

"Yes he would, and that's that!" Madan Horace servilely agreed.

"It's the rich who enable the poor to live," the sheriff continued. "You cultivate your peas, you plant your corn. Good. But isn't it necessary for the rich to take all that from your hands, that they buy it from you, so that you can pay for a pair of pants and a shirt? For you can't go walking around naked. And if you respect society, whenever you go down to town you've got to wear shoes. We are poor people, I agree, but that doesn't mean at all that we are vagabonds and infidels."

Charles shook his head.

"What you've just said there, Constable Delisca, was a fine speech. I won't deny it. But the rich also need the poor. When Master Morin wants to build his fence, will he not be obliged to call on his hired man to do it for him? If he needs to carry a load to town, must he not turn to Desilus or some other farm laborer, since, in his own position, it wouldn't do for him to carry it down himself on his own head?"

The justice of the peace wouldn't admit he was stumped.

"Respect is what makes society," he affirmed sententiously. "And it's for that reason, don't you see, that there is the law. The spring belongs to Master Morin, so he has the right to do what he wants with it."

"Now that's just where I can't agree with you, Constable. Why should Master Morin be allowed to do whatever he pleases with the spring? God himself gave water to living Christians, so that they might drink when they are thirsty. The water does not belong to Master Morin."

"Yes, Charles, what you say there is very true. But who made the law? Who wanted to have both the rich and the poor on earth? Isn't it also the Good Lord? My child, I am old; look upon my head."

He raised his helmet again and showed his almost completely grey hair to the young man.

"Heed my advice. If you don't want life to treat you badly, behave well towards the rich. You see, Master Morin is really not at all a bad fellow. I grant that perhaps he's hotheaded, and sometimes he talks big. But he's a man who loves law and order above everything. And that's why I will surely get along well with him."

ossuet accompanied Morin back to his farm and immediately said good-bye. As he walked away, the hired man stopped working to look after him, then shook his head. But he said nothing, and Morin became worried.

"What's wrong, Desilus?"

The hired man paused in his work, leaned on the crowbar and lowered his eyes.

"Mist' Dutilleul, it isn't that I want to speak ill of any man to you. But—I ask God to pardon me!—that Bossuet you see there, he is not a Negro whom you can trust, no sir."

"Desilus, what you say doesn't make sense. Isn't Bossuet the godfather of your son?"

"Yes, Mist' Dutilleul," he admitted with a deep sigh. "That's him, the godfather of my own little boy."

"And you talk to me about him in this way!"

"But you had a right to know, Mist' Dutilleul. In the days gone by old folk used to say that you had to sleep with John to know how John snores. Very well, it's true that Bossuet is the godfather of my son. It's also true that he never harmed me, directly. But believe me, I can't work for you that way. I am the hired man on your farm. I see you do an imprudent thing. And then you expect me to say nothing about it? No, none of that for me! Oh, no, no! That's impossible! As for Bossuet, you must hear me out. It's true that he is neither a better nor a worse Negro than any other. Nevertheless, I know he doesn't like you. He doesn't like you, not at all!"

"And who do you think you're talking to, Desilus? You seem to think that I'm still a little babe in the cradle who can't see yet."

"Oh, no, Mist' Dutilleul, I could never believe that. It's true that I've never been educated. But I'm not stupid. You know how to read and write. I don't know any of those things. Then how can I dare to believe that you are not a practical man? But, without showing any lack of respect for you, I will tell you that there are things which one cannot learn from books."

"And what are those things, Desilus?"

"Oh, there are loads of them, Mist' Dutilleul, loads and loads of them. . . . Excuse me if I remind you that you come from the city and you don't yet know the ways of country folk. But I was born here, and I know everybody in Musseau. If I tell you to be careful with Bossuet, I know what I'm talking about."

"But what harm could he do me, Desilus? Assassinate me? I have my revolver and I'm not afraid of him. He need only come. . . . Just take a look at this."

Morin drew his revolver from its holster on his belt, where he wore it for all to see, aimed at a mango and shot the fruit off its stem.

"You see, Desilus? Very well, that's the way I'd pick him off, your Bossuet. He need only come looking for trouble, I tell you, and that's what he'll get."

"Mist' Dutilleul, as for shooting, you're good, and that's not bluffing. No, you sure know how to shoot! And if anyone should attack you, your gun will be a great help, there's no doubt of that. But, ai-ai-ai! Boss, believe me, that's not the way Bossuet will come, no sir! He's too smart for that. With the help of evil spirits he could send you a run of hard luck, sickness and even death. And if you have to deal with evil spirits then even rifles, machine guns, cannon would be useless to protect you."

"Desilus, I don't fear your evil spirits, believe me. The spirits only exist for the gullible minds of ignorant Negroes like yourself."

"That's so, Mist' Dutilleul. What you say there is true. And I myself have already admitted to you that I've never gone to school. But Bossuet, he's different. He does know how to read and write. He has influential friends, high-placed people in Port-au-Prince, and the spirits he serves are not the humble spirits of poor, ignorant Negroes like myself."

Strange things happened at Musseau. Bossuet often would disappear for a week or two. One fine morning he would reappear, as if by magic, in the middle of his garden. Sometimes he reappeared in the middle of the night, and he would be driven up in the luxurious car of some rich man.

People said that the automobile belonged to a well-known lawyer friend of his, whom public gossip accused of practicing witchcraft. As a matter of fact, that rumor made up a good part of his prestige, and added to his clientele. But the extraordinary fear that Bossuet inspired in the farmers was based on a story that he himself had told them at a party one night when he was drunk. It was an incredible story, in which he explained his long absences. He made out that he often went to the Forban Gorge on the Saint Mark highway.

The impressionable description that Bossuet had given of the ill-famed grottoes certainly did not conform to the truth about them as revealed by learned archeologists; but it did confirm, in every detail, the popular legend of the Forban Gorge, and that was enough to convince the poor people of Musseau that he was speaking the truth.

According to him, to enter the place you had to ask permission from the spirits who guarded it. First you had to write them a letter, explaining the purpose of the visit, and place it under a big stone at the entrance of the cavern. Then you had to return the following evening at nightfall. There stood a beautiful woman with fascinating eyes, black as the bottom of a cauldron, naked and silent. She would take you by the hand and lead you into the dwelling place of the infernal spirits.

For a long time you would walk in pitch blackness, over soft and humid earth. At last you reached a large cavern filled with a strange twilight glow which came from nowhere, but suffused the air. The woman would drop your hand and utter a terrified shriek, which would split and roll and prolong itself in that confined space like a terrible clap of thunder.

At this strange summons, an amazing creature, called the Cigouave, would rise up before you. It was impossible to see where it came from. The Cigouave is neither man nor beast, although it seems to be made up of both. Its body resembles that of a large wild dog and is about the size of an ass. But it has the head and feet of a man, with long fanged teeth. It does not speak. It howls and barks like a dog and the woman acts as its interpreter.

She transmits your request to the Cigouave in an unknown tongue, and then translates the conditions it lays down. And when an agreement is reached, she makes an incision in your arm with the sharp point of a knife, in the shape of a cross, draws blood from it with her left index finger and traces cabalistic signs on the earth. That seals the pact.

Immediately you find yourself plunged in a profound twilight filled with blinding flashes of lightning, you hear the roll of thunder and the sharp whistling of a violent wind, you are lifted from the earth and borne away by some mysterious force. Finally you lose all sense of time or place, and when you regain your senses you are far from the grotto, lying across a path at the haunted crossroads of two paths. . . .

That was the story Bossuet told, and Desilus transmitted it faithfully to Morin Dutilleul, who, naturally, didn't believe a single word of it.

"Very well, Mist' Dutilleul," said the hired hand, "and I suppose if I were to tell you the story of Ferdinand, maybe you would think that was a joke too?"

"Ferdinand? Which Ferdinand?"

Desilus told him Ferdinand was a young brother of Bossuet Metelus, who, when alive, had lived in Port-au-Prince. There he had established a good position for himself through his own hard efforts. From infancy his parents had left him to live with well-to-do people. As he was an intelligent boy, and gifted in his studies, his masters, satisfied by his conduct, sent him to school every afternoon as soon as work in the house was finished.

When he was old enough to learn a trade, they got him a job in a garage. He lost no time in becoming a skilled mechanic and chauffeur. A fellow of real merit, yes sir, was this Ferdinand, and serious on top of it! And honest! A young man the likes of which you don't often meet these days. Well, he was boldly making his own way in life. Mechanical things held no secrets from him. And so, in less than three years he had put aside enough money to buy a truck and to work on his own account. As he earned a lot with the truck, soon he was able to buy a house, and then he got married.

One day, nobody seems to know the reason why, Ferdinand came to see Bossuet. Before that he used to visit him only on rare occasions. He was told his brother was in the garden. He looked for him in vain. As he was returning to the house he noticed, under the trees which lined the ravine, a strange little hut. It was there, people said, that Bossuet used to go to study magic in books written by white Frenchmen, books with odd names like *Albert the Great* and *Red Dragon*.

Ferdinand boldly entered the hut. Nobody ever learned what took place there between the two brothers, but soon after Ferdinand, who up to that day had never touched even a drop of rum, began to drink heavily. He never went back to work again, and ran into debt, so that in the end, after he had sold both his truck and his house, his wife left him.

One morning he was found hanging from a tree, near that evil hut he had entered to his own downfall.

"Mist' Dutilleul," Desilus concluded, "if you ever return to Bossuet's house for any reason whatsoever, never go that way!"

"Enough, Desilus!" Morin sharply interrupted him. Then, as he turned to go, "You will do better to work instead of telling such ridiculous stories, and giving free advice to those who aren't asking for it!"

"Yes, sir, Mist' Dutilleul!" Desilus bent down to dig the earth again.

As he entered the house, a wave of lassitude overwhelmed Morin Dutilleul. The tales of his hired man, despite his natural scepticism, troubled him not a little. He had a great desire to lie down on the fresh, cool bricks of the veranda floor, to fall asleep and descend into those obscure depths where dreams never reach. But, afraid that if he did so he would lower himself in the eyes of his servants, he did not give way to his desire.

Decidedly, he thought, one can do nothing good with such brutes!

If there were only some way to destroy in them the inept beliefs which obscured their understanding. . . . But it was becoming clear to Morin that they held to those very beliefs more than to their own skins. And he asked himself if their superstitions were not the product of an innate stupidity, for it seemed to him that they had been endowed with them once and for all, and that they could never be rooted out.

His bitterness as he pondered these unfair thoughts was stronger because he knew how false such reasoning could be. And he was annoyed by the realization that these superstititons were so strongly rooted because those of his own class had taken no serious steps to improve the pitiful living conditions of the Haitian peasants.

As he entered the dining room the sound of footsteps on the stairway caused him to look up. The maid was coming down from the garret, a pitcher in her hands. This seemed unusual, for it was almost noon and she should have finished cleaning his room a long time ago. Furthermore, the table was already set. . . . A suspicion darted through his mind that she had only taken the pitcher to justify her presence in his room, at a time when she had no reason to be there. But then what could have attracted her to his room?

"Sinette, come here," he sternly ordered.

She came up to him, surprised and intimidated.

"What were you doing up there at this hour?"

"Nothing, sir, nothing, I was only going to fill the pitcher at the spring! I forgot to do it this morning."

"Let me have it!"

She held it out to him. Contrary to his expectations, the pitcher was empty. Still he pretended to be furious, and frowned at her.

"Very well," he said between clenched teeth. "But make sure it doesn't happen again. Do you hear?"

"Yes, sir," she said timidly.

She went out of the house with lowered head, filled with sadness and submission. Morin shrugged his shoulders. Obviously he had made a mistake in sleeping with this girl. It had become painful, since then, to command her, for Sinette was hardly lazy in her passion, as his flesh ardently remembered.

She was an attractive Negress. Clean, tall, carved with vigor, she had provocative breasts and buttocks, and her lips were plump and violet like the skin of a ripe fig. In her glance gleamed the sparkle of which the Haitian poet Oswald Durand has sung, "like glowing candles are her eyes"—a creole image which the night of her body fully justified.

One evening in a state of intense excitation, Morin Dutilleul had gone to her in the dining room, where she slept on a matting on the floor. He had taken her almost without resistance; but the next day what he had done disturbed him as an act of infidelity to the memory of Eugenie. Seized with remorse, he swore never to sleep with her again, and although his continence troubled him, he stuck to his word from then on.

Naturally, Sinette, who was already calculating the advantages she might gain from a liaison with her master, was surprised and deceived by his distant reserve. She was unable to reconcile herself to this change, and for several nights she would climb up to the garret after Morin was in bed.

"Did Master call me?" she would ask shyly.

Or she would knock on his door and call out: "Does Master need anything?"

But each time, although he was fully aroused upon seeing her trembling there before him in her nightgown, Morin had angrily sent her away. . . . She lay on the hard mat and sobbed to herself all night.

When she reached the spring, Sinette placed the jug under the bamboo overflow pipe and leaning against the mound, she held her head in her hands and wept.

"Ho-ho!" Desilus, whom she had not seen standing nearby, exclaimed in surprise. "Why, what's wrong with you?"

Sinette, embarrassed that someone had seen her, wiped her eyes hastily with the hem of her skirt.

"It's nothing, Desilus, nothing. I just had a great longing to see my mother."

"Well, well! Imagine that! And I was afraid that Mist' Dutilleul had said something harsh to you."

"Well, yes, there was also that. I expected it anyway, and I wouldn't be surprised if he should order me out of the house one of these days. This morning, while I was combing my hair, a black butterfly lit on my shoulder. As I reached up to brush him off, my mirror fell and broke into tiny splinters."

Desilus clucked his tongue.

"And you didn't cleanse the room with a pail of water, at once?"

Sinette, so choked with emotion she was unable to speak, nodded no.

"So now, my daughter, now you're in a real fix! If I were in your place I wouldn't lose a moment's time, but rush off to consult a witch doctor, one of the best houngans."

"But don't you know that I'm a practicing Catholic, that I go to Communion regularly?"

"You've told me that before. Only I assure you that no Communion is going to get you out of the tough spot you're in now. And never forget, believe me, you can desert the pagan gods, but the loas, they will never renounce you or leave you. At the very moment when you least expect it, all the worst things can happen to you. And you may be sure that it's the spirits whom you have renounced who will inflict them on you as a punishment."

"I know that very well," Sinette admitted, meekly lowering her eyes, discouraged. "But . . ."

She never completed her thought, saying to herself that Desilus was surely right and that she had no other recourse than the one he had indicated to save herself from some terrible calamity.

t was a morning warm with the softness of spring. The sunlight, filtered by a breeze, powdered the plateau with an incandescent pollen. The stealthy laziness which precedes the midday stupor of the tropics crept over the countryside. Only the mocking bird, defying the rapacity of the carrion crows, still praised the sparkling splendor of the light with its thrilling song. Already one could hear the patient gnawing of the termites in the planks of the wooden shack, precursors of the hot and silent hours.

As usual, despite the buzzing and tickling of the flies, Madan Horace dozed behind the counter of her shop, in perfect harmony with the outside world. Charles, on the contrary, showed himself insensible to the insistent urge of his surroundings. Seated on the edge of the porch, he drew angry puffs from his short-stemmed clay pipe.

He was thinking of Irma, his fiancée, and the indecent proposals that Bossuet had made to her in Petionville market place where he had encountered her the day before. He recalled the details which the young girl had told him between sobs. She had taken his hand in hers and implored him with her eyes to understand. She made no effort to wipe away the tears which rolled down from her almond eyes, staining the dusky bloom of her tender face, and this image aroused his anger even more than her halting words. He had instantly sworn to avenge the insult.

"You know," she went on, "you know . . . he . . . he even wanted to take me by force."

"The bastard!" Charles muttered in a low voice. "The bastard, he'll pay for that, I swear to you! For I'm not a weakling like Ferdinand, who'll get sentimental and hang myself. It's Bossuet who must die that way. I'm not an idiot, thank God, and he'll soon learn that the last child from our mother's womb was stronger than the others she bore!"

Thus had Ti-Charles spoken, but he still had not figured out how to induce the guilty man to commit suicide. Bossuet was, in his opinion, one of the most accomplished practitioners of the art of witchcraft in the whole land. And this feeling of inferiority to his elder brother only heightened the young man's rage.

Horace, who was puttering around the yard, finally became astonished at his moody silence:

"Oh, Charles," he called. "What's wrong with you today? We haven't heard a peep out of you all morning."

"What's the use of talking, Horace? Only the knife can know what is in the heart of the yam!"

"Ho-ho, my child, what's that you're saying? Has someone done you wrong?"

The young man shrugged his shoulders. Madan Horace, awakened with a start, stared stupidly at him.

"What is wrong then, little brother?" she asked.

"I'll tell you, sis, but you will hardly be willing to believe me. Yesterday afternoon Bossuet tried to induce Irma to go out with him. He wanted to sleep with her!"

"Our Bossuet?" Her voice was horrified.

"Bossuet himself, in person, Madan Horace! Without the slightest shame, he offered to build her a little cabin and to set her up in business with a stock of merchandise. And then . . . then he tried to violate her!"

"Do you believe, Ti-Charles, that it could possibly be true?"

"Do I believe it? But Irma herself told me!"

"Now isn't that sad, my friends?" the carpenter exclaimed. "Tell me, isn't Bossuet old enough to think of his self-respect? But alas, there you see what happens to a man when he does not live in the faith of the Lord. . . ."

Cherisena came up running. Horace, sensing something abnormal, fell silent. The child, excited, went to stand before the shopkeeper.

"Oh, godmother! Master Morin has gone completely crazy, yes, ma'am! He has just cut down the mapou tree by the spring!"

"The altar of the Almighty Legba!" groaned the shopkeeper, her eyes wide with terror.

But Ti-Charles was triumphant.

"There you are, there you are! Didn't I tell you only the other day that that man would make us see every color of the rainbow? You remember, Madan Horace, that Justice Delice assured me Master Morin had no other intention than to restore order on his own property. So now, my friends, which of us was right? Now all the women with child may well hold their bellies and scream, for evil days have fallen upon us. Mark my words!"

"We are the children of the Lord," the carpenter raised his eyes piously to the heavens. "His will be done, on earth as it is in heaven!"

Madan Horace made the sign of the cross. Ti-Charles spat on the ground to show his disgust, outraged by their utter resignation, which he considered revolting cowardice. He stood up, hitched his pants with a resolute gesture and without taking leave of the couple strode off in the direction of the spring.

On the way he encountered Sor Cie, Bossuet's wife, running towards him like a madwoman, holding her head with both hands and uttering sharp, hysterical cries. As soon as she encountered her brother-in-law she broke down in sobs.

"My child," she gasped puffing, "did you hear the terrible news? Someone has just chopped down Papa Legba's tree!"

Charles looked at her coldly.

"And what has Bossuet to say about that?"

"Bossuet, my poor little one! But what would you expect him to do? Master Morin always carries his pistol on his hip. And then, tell me, isn't a man who does not fear to chop down the altar of a god the very devil incarnate?"

The young man pondered, silent a moment.

"Good, Sor Cie. But there's one thing I don't understand. Why should Master Morin do such a thing?"

"Why, Ti-Charles, don't you know?"

She wrung her hands.

"He did it because this morning he found a food offering which Bossuet and I had just placed at the foot of the mapou tree in honor of Legba. He declared that the tree, growing on his side of the brook, was his property. Since it belonged to him he could not tolerate such lawlessness on our part. He would make sure it could not happen again. . . ."

Madan Bossuet had already aroused the entire countryside. By the time Ti-Charles reached the spring, a crowd of cowed peasants contemplated the disaster in silence. The mapou tree had fallen its full length along the stream-bed, and, as if to fulfill the proverb, the little kids of Musseau were already nibbling at its leaves.

Without paying the slightest attention to the country folk herded on the opposite bank, Morin Dutilleul, aided by his faithful Desilus, was busily fencing in the spring. The hired man was digging holes, putting in the fence posts, stamping the earth back with his bare feet, while his master strung the barbed wire. And so Morin's warning, emerging from the dimness of a hypothetical future, took shape before the eyes of the peasants, and moved towards completion as implacably as fate.

This was too much for Ti-Charles, whose nerves had been keyed to the tension of a powerless rage since the evening before.

"May lightning strike me dead!" he swore aloud, enraged. "We cannot be deprived of water because of one man's whim!"

Guessing the state of mind he was in, and fearing that he might do something to start a riot, the justice of the peace tried to calm him. But he only succeeded in turning the young man's wrath against himself.

"So you think, Constable," he snarled, "that Master Morin will throw you a little bone to gnaw, for taking his side against everyone else? Can't you see what he's up to? Every time he needs you he'll grin at you with every tooth in his head. After that he'll give you a good swift kick in the tail, for that's the way dogs are always thanked for their pains."

It was a bitter pill for Delisca Delice to swallow before all those people. He thought he would suffocate with shame, for he could not forget that he was justice of the peace "under his own command," as he sometimes put it. "Beware, Ti-Charles," he said severely. "Remember that it's the law itself you are insulting with those words."

"You! You the law! Permit me to laugh in your face. Let me point out to you that there is only one chief in these parts. And it's not you, but Master Morin. He's the one who lays down the law as he sees fit. It certainly isn't you."

"Ti-Charles! Keep quiet or I'll make you keep quiet. Yes I will!"

"Me, Constable? Just try it once, and you'll learn what it can cost you. And now I'm going to show you that I'm not afraid of Master Morin either."

So saying, he strode across the fence, ripped up one of the stakes that Desilus had just planted and threw it to the ground. Morin grabbed his revolver and menacingly took aim. Ti-Charles instinctively recoiled, but kept up his vocal show of courage.

"Shoot me, Master Morin! Shoot if you dare!"

And so, to show the natives his determination to be tough, but taking care not to hit him, Morin fired over his head. An indescribable panic followed. Everybody, including Ti-Charles and Constable Delice, took to their heels. But the justice of the peace didn't go far. As soon as he recovered from his fright, he walked back to find Morin.

"Master," he said ingratiatingly, "I compliment you on your firmness. Only there was no need for you to shoot at us like that. I myself was on the point of restoring order."

"Ah, were you?" Morin sarcastically remarked. "So you

weren't really with the others against me? Very well, then, tell me why you ran away like the rest of them?"

"Master, I thought you were going to shoot at all of us. You seemed in such an angry mood. But how could I be on the side of the farmers, when the law is on your side?"

"Enough!" Morin cut him off, annoyed. "In my opinion you talk too much. I have other things to do besides listening to your explanations. Desilus, let's get back to work."

"Master, I am leaving," the constable announced timidly, after a moment's hesitation. "Yes, I don't want to disturb you . . ."

Morin didn't even deign to answer him. He was proud of having gotten the upper hand of the peasants so easily and thought it wise to show Delisca again that he did not need him around to make himself respected in Musseau.

Desilus marveled at his show of nerve.

"Mist' Dutilleul, you are a man, yes, sir! You don't wear pants for nothing!"

Morin suppressed a fatuous smile.

"Let's get to work, Desilus," he said dryly. "It's already late and it will soon be time for lunch."

All those who had fled gathered at Horace's general store to comment on these events.

"Master Morin will meet a bad end one of these days," one of them declared. "A man who does not fear the gods, indeed! Tell me, wasn't that his own grave he was digging under his feet?"

"As a matter of fact," said the shopkeeper, "I'm afraid he doesn't realize what kind of a man he's up against in Bossuet. Whenever anyone dares to take him on—"

Ti-Charles, annoyed, interrupted her.

"Bah! And who is he anyway, your Bossuet? Nothing but an old rotten tooth, which can pretend it's strong only when nibbling at bananas! He only does wrong when he's dealing with black Negroes, his own people. As for dealing with rich mulattos like Master Morin, they need only raise their voices in his presence and he bows his head, ready to excuse himself. That's what he's really like."

"In that case," said the shopkeeper, "isn't there anyone here to defend the rights of us poor wretched Negroes?"

"No, Madan Horace, there isn't! I won't say that we've settled our accounts with Master Morin yet. But if we wait for Bossuet to settle them, he'll live to a hundred years old, believe me."

"Don't say such things, Ti-Charles, don't. Whenever anyone does something against Bossuet and he says nothing, that's the time to fear him most. . . . You know as well as I do that Bossuet has great powers of magic."

"That's what you believe anyway. But as for me, Madan Horace, I'll wager you that our brother has no powers except in stealing wives away from the peasants or doing them harm in some other way. He can exert no more power over Master Morin than a child can at its mother's breast."

The carpenter, joining his hands, raised his eyes to heaven.

"Almighty Lord, leave not your children . . ."

At these words Irma, standing beside her lover, took him softly by the arm.

"Ti-Charles, I'm going home now. Won't you go with me? I have something to tell you."

"What's wrong now?" the young man asked in a worried tone. "It isn't Bossuet again?"

"I'll tell you on the way."

"All right, let's go then." He was impatient to know what she had to tell him.

"Ti-Charles," she said, when they were far enough away not to be seen or heard by anyone. "Don't bother yourself about Bossuet."

"But why shouldn't I fix him, Irma? Didn't he try to seduce you away from me?"

"Of course, but since you know that he's only wasting his time, what harm can he do to us? If I feel this way about it now, it's simply because I'm afraid for your life. Just look how close Master Morin came to killing you a little while ago. I'm frightened for you."

She really feared that by starting a battle with Bossuet her lover might meet the same fate as Ferdinand. Touched by her emotion and the tenderness she showed him, Ti-Charles put his arms around the girl, drew her ardently to him and held her in a powerful and passionate embrace. She bit his lip lightly, then drew back; but she had grown dizzy in his arms and had to lean against her lover to keep from fainting. He tried to embrace her again.

"No, Ti-Charles," she begged softly. "I must get back to the house. I have to finish the laundry. . . . Will you come tonight?"

"You know very well I'll come. How could I keep away? I feel lost when I am not beside you."

"And I count the minutes until I see you again. But you must promise me that you won't try to do anything to Bossuet."

"I'll try, Irma, only because you ask me. But if he dares to go chasing around after you again I won't be able to answer for myself."

lthough he was broken by fatigue that night Desilus twisted and turned on his mat, tortured by fear. The sacrilege Morin had committed that morning, in forcing him to chop down the mapou tree consecrated to Legba, made him fear the dire retribution that it would call down upon the inhabitants of Musseau. And he had no doubt that calamity would be unleashed particularly against himself, redoubling the problems of one already haunted by an evil fate.

Of course he refused to be the first to strike the tree, believing the proverb that he who shouts "Here is the adder!" is the one who truly kills it. He had insisted that Morin himself wield the first two blows of the ax against the sacred tree. But that certainly would not soften the anger of the loas, for when avenging an insult to their prestige they did not even make any distinction between the innocent and the guilty. They always struck blindly against men, or animals, or plants and sometimes even the earth itself. Only those protected by powerful spirits sometimes escaped from their wild fury.

However, poor Desilus already had his hands full trying to protect himself from his son. There was such a parallel between his own progressive decline and his son's growing vigor that he suspected that his son visited him in the night to suck his blood and marrow like a werewolf, as he slept.

At first he had considered strangling his son. But then he feared this might only turn against him the hostility of the spirit of the boy's mother who had died only two years before. Moreover, he also feared the justice of his fellow men, who he knew were never tender when judging the acts of the poor. Finally, hoping that separation would protect him, he had sent his son away to Petionville to live with his maternal grandparents. Alas, the move proved vain; his strength continued to ebb from him, even more swiftly than before.

Terror-stricken, he had prayed to his dead wife, beseeching the woman who had been so good to him when she was alive, to come and bear her son away to the great beyond. Every day he visited her grave, blessed it with generous libations, and once each week he would make a blood sacrifice of a chicken to her. At last one night his dead spouse appeared to him in a dream.

"Oh, Desilus, I beg you to cease these prayers to me!" she pleaded. "What you ask of me is not honest! If you knew how much I suffer because of your shameful thoughts . . ."

No, decidedly, he could expect no help from the spirits.

Tonight, as if to justify his fears, a devilish wind howled, clawing at the earth. And through the warped boards of the door, which the storm rattled and shook, he saw continually the vibrant glow of lightning. The cabin, shaken violently by the tempest, creaked in every board as if it might be torn apart at any moment. Then came the sudden rush of the downpour. He heard it at a great distance like a huge drum pounding the jungle vegetation and the earth. The sound rose to a roar and in an instant burst upon him. All the water of the heavens seemed to fall down in a flood upon the earth, with the power and fury of an avalanche, amid the din of thunder.

There could be no more doubt. These were only the external signs of the great discontent of the gods. . . .

And in the main house neither Sinette nor Morin was able to sleep. The maid was prey to the same superstitious terrors as Desilus; while the master, his anger cooled, saw with foreboding the possible reactions of the peasants, and of Bossuet in particular. Would they not try to poison him? These country people knew the terrible secret of venomous plants, and were skilled in making use of it in the most subtle and hidden ways. What could he do to ward off such a danger?

Up to now his servants were without doubt faithful to him. But might not the resentment of Sinette, nourished by each passing day, influence her to place herself at the service of his enemies? And as for Desilus, otherwise so loyal, so devoted, could he not easily be won over by adroitly putting pressure on him through his foolish superstitions? These and similar questions tormented Morin Dutilleul.

In his quandary, he had already drunk half a bottle of rum. Stimulated by alcohol, his imagination gradually began to run wild; images and ideas crashed together in his mind, and broke into disjointed fragments, multiplied themselves, until they were finally jumbled into a chaotic nightmare. Soon a splitting headache pounded in his skull, seized his temples in a vice as though forcing them into a steel helmet. He poured water on his head and took an aspirin tablet. Then, blowing out the lamp, he went to bed. But his torment persisted.

He had in fact committed two stupid blunders. . . . Why? . . . Yes, why had he made love to Sinette? . . .

Perhaps his drinking had been a partial cause. . . . Yes, perhaps . . . But was there not also the memory of the black washerwomen of the Wood-of-Oaks, whose bare thighs had troubled his childhood in the distant past?

And the second blunder, the mapou tree by the spring, what strange whim had forced him to order Desilus to chop it down? . . . There was no good reason, except his inability to resist the slightest impulse of his violent nature . . . . The warm blood of the tropics. . . . Yes, it was indeed that!

When the downpour abruptly ceased, the fresh, humid night was filled with the croaking of a thousand tree toads. They chanted their relief from the oppressive heat with a vile concert of harsh voices, in which a grating bass chorus answered the theme sung by a shrill soloist. Morin felt a horror of those clammy little beasts. He could stand them no longer. In a fit of temper he got up, relit the lamp and poured himself a large bumper of rum, which he swallowed in one gulp; then he paced the room, nervous and uneasy.

To dismiss the maid and Desilus would perhaps be the right solution. . . . But their substitutes might be even more dangerous. . . . Sleep with Sinette once more? . . . Ah, no! Anything but not that! He had no taste for the promiscuity to which liaisons with one's servants fatally lead. . . . Moreover, there must surely be some other way to conciliate her . . . A few little gifts might do . . . Why not? . . . More politeness in his commands to her . . . A raise in wages . . . Yes, especially the latter. He would use the same tactics on Desilus . . . And also keep a sharp eye on both of them. . . . And in everything he did, he must remain carefully suspicious of them, without ever letting it become obvious. . . . But as for Bossuet there was only one way. He must break with him completely, and without wasting any time in useless pretense.

Little by little the headache left him. Now he felt light, full of flexibility and agility. And in this artificial sense of well-being, the future appeared smooth and easy to him. But, to achieve this state of bliss he had completely emptied the entire bottle. Without realizing it, he opened another. . . .

Morin's agitation had not escaped the notice of Sinette, who listened with uneasy curiosity to his restless pacing to and fro in the garret overhead, asking herself what could be wrong with her master to keep him up at this late hour. Could it be that the offended god already tormented him, as a prelude to his implacable vengeance, when he would drive him into total insanity? It was not long before she was certain of this, when for the first time since she had been in his employ she heard him sing. What convinced her above all was the hymn he sang in the thick and grotesquely mournful voice he had learned when he frequented the cabarets. It was the lugubrious chant from the mass for the dead:

> Dies irae, dies illa,
> Crucis expandens vexilla,
> Solvet seclum in favilla. . . .

How had these words ever come to him, Sinette asked herself with horror, since he never went to church and

believed neither in God nor the devil? He was surely possessed! The vengeance of Legba had already begun to
work on him!

Morin continued his pacing in the garret, but his steps
became heavy, uncertain, and from time to time he
stumbled against the furniture in the room. Finally he
halted.

"He's still drinking!" Sinette sighed, shivering.

Suddenly she sat bolt upright on her pallet; there was
the noise of a collapsing body, then not a sound, only
silence and the black night, and fear!

Hurriedly she threw open the outer door and shouted:

"Oh, Desilus! Hurry! Come quickly! Mast' Dutilleul
is ill!"

The hired man arrived, puffing.

"What has upset you like this, Sinette?"

"I really don't know what's happened. But Mast' Dutilleul was pacing around in the garret and he was singing a
funeral dirge when all of a sudden I heard him fall in a
heap on the floor."

"Ho-ho! Ho-ho! You don't mean that, Sinette? What
can you be saying?"

"Should we go up and see what's happened to him?"

"Do you think we should, Sinette? . . . But suppose
there's nothing wrong with Mist' Dutilleul, how will he
take it? You know him! He's a man who never makes a
joke. He doesn't spread any butter with his machete, as
they say."

"But I tell you, with my own two ears I heard him fall
down."

"What a fix!" groaned Desilus, annoyed.

Then, abruptly making up his mind:

"Since that's the way it is, we should go up and see what has happened up there. Only Sinette, I warn you, if there's nothing wrong with Mist' Dutilleul and he gets mad, it's you who'll be responsible when he asks why we entered his room. . . ."

They found Morin stretched out on the floor, his eyes closed like a corpse and his arms flung wide, as though stretched on a cross. Desilus looked at the empty bottle and understood at once.

"If there isn't a sad sight, Sinette! Can you tell me why a man of wealth like Mist' Dutilleul should get himself in such a state as this? . . . But he himself, by his own stubbornness, asked for it. I warned him well that Bossuet would do him wrong. He wouldn't listen to me. He made me chop down the mapou tree of All Merciful Legba . . . And now, just look at that! . . . Just see how he has been struck down. It's all his own fault!"

Aided by Sinette, Desilus carried Morin back to his bed. Then the maid rubbed his face with half a lemon and put cold compresses on his head. He seemed finally to revive and shortly he was snoring gently, but his breath came in short gasps, as though something still oppressed him. . . .

"Ah, Sinette!" sighed Desilus when they were back in the dining room. "This fit wasn't natural, not at all. It's true that Mist' Dutilleul is in the habit of drinking; but never, never have I seen him get into such a state as that. It must be that some evil spirit now haunts him."

"Oh, don't say that, Desilus, please!"

"But why not, Sinette? It must be so, otherwise how can you explain what's just happened to him?"

"Oh, Desilus, you can't be right. Mast' Dutilleul is a man of social standing. How then could an evil spirit be after him? Only poor, unfortunate people like us are accursed by evil spirits."

"That's what you think, Sinette. But you forget that he forced me to chop down the mapou tree beside the spring this morning. You also forget that many well-to-do people have long ago abandoned faith in their family gods. Just because they sometimes have a lighter skin than ours, they forget that they too are children of Yayoute, our common African ancestor, and assume they have no more obligations toward the gods. But the loas never forget what is their due.

"Just see what's happening to you too. At first Mist' Dutilleul had only sweet words for you. Then, one fine day, just like that, he goes to bed with you. He takes you, and afterwards what happens? Although you did him no wrong, he can no longer stand the sight of you. You're even lucky that he hasn't yet kicked you out of his house and home. Tell me, do you think that would have happened to you if you had not abandoned your family gods and taken Holy Communion? Otherwise wouldn't you today be the mistress of this house, here and now?"

Sinette sighed.

"Now listen to me," he said to her. "One of these days I'm going to consult Rossini, the voodoo priest of Bourdon. If you want, I'll explain your case to him. . . ."

They talked of these things until early dawn. Then Desilus yawned, stretched his arms and scratched his ribs.

"I'm going out to milk the cows," he announced sleepily.

 oungan Rossini lived in a most peculiar house. It had none of the character of a peasant's home. Perched on the summit of Bourdon hill, it overlooked the macadam highway that led to Petionville, and seemed more like a dovecote than a house. In fact, no one would have been astonished if pigeons had flown out of the tiny windows of the upper room. That, at least, had always been the hope of Desilus every time that he passed by the house, for, despite the instability of his precarious life, his imagination had remained childish and whimsical.

Although this was not his first visit, he nevertheless felt uneasy when he knocked on the door of Rossini's house that day.

A gnomelike hunchback, his head hanging grotesquely on one side and grinning with the frightful fixed smile of an idiot, opened the door for him and led him to a chair. He was an abandoned child whom the houngan had adopted, certainly not from charity but in order to impress his devotees; and as he expected, they did not fail to regard the dwarf as a supernatural being, an evil spirit which the voodoo priest had domesticated to serve his magic purposes.

Making a grotesque bow with his crooked legs, the urchin disappeared behind a palm matting which formed a frail barrier separating the living room from the dining room. Rossini himself soon appeared from behind it, serious and inscrutable, and as imposing as the Archbishop of

Port-au-Prince. He seemed aged, with his white hair and his small, greying beard; but his firm and straight bearing showed that great vigor remained in him.

He ceremoniously offered two fingers to Desilus and then sank down comfortably into a rocking chair.

"What news do you bring?" he asked.

Desilus sighed.

"Since you find me back at your house, Rossini, can't you guess that things are not going well for me?"

"So I see, Desilus. . . . You know how to put things, and always speak to the point. But you're all the same. You never come to see me until you find yourselves in hot water. While things are going well with you, you neglect your family gods. They must always punish you before you will think of them."

He sighed, then looking Desilus straight in the eyes, he said:

"What you came for has something to do with your son?"

"Yes, it concerns him. He is draining me of all my strength . . ."

"I know that, Desilus, just from looking at you. . . . Very well, now let's see. How long has it been since you offered food to the gods?"

Desilus nervously scratched his head, as though that might summon an answer.

"Now let me see . . . it must have been about two years ago, wouldn't you say, Rossini? The last time I came it was about my wife, who had just died."

"That's right, Desilus, two years ago. But what could you possibly have been doing all the time since then, to dare neglect the loas of your family?"

"What have I been doing! . . . You must understand, Rossini, I am only a poor miserable wretch."

"You haven't been working all that time?"

"Well, I have steady work now, but only since Mist' Dutilleul came to settle down in Musseau. Before that I only worked at odd jobs here and there, whenever I was lucky enough to find one. I've lived my whole life like that, and I've never been able to save a penny."

"What about your vegetable garden?"

"My garden, Rossini? You call that scrawny patch of ground a garden? Why, it has never furnished me with anything except a few ears of corn, and two or three sacks of potatoes; just enough to cheat hunger for a few days."

"You want me to believe that, Desilus? You know how to earn money all right. But when you get your hands on money, what do you do with it? You throw it away in gambling, and whatever luckily remains after that, you drink it down, or you smoke it into thin air!"

"Oh, no, Rossini! If you hear tales about some men who always gamble, don't count me among them. It's been a long time, a very long time, since I've rolled dice."

"All right, I'd like to believe you. However, if you were to put aside a little of the money you throw away on drinks and smokes each year, wouldn't you have enough to offer a little religious service to your family loas? But no, you prefer to wait until evil times have fallen upon you, before you come looking for me. I wonder if it isn't already too late to fix things up. Look at the sorry mess you've put yourself in."

Desilus bowed his head, discouraged.

"Now, then, who are your family gods?" asked Rossini.

"Let me see. Ogoun is your guardian spirit, isn't he?"

"Yes, it's Ogoun."

"Very well, then. You'd better come back to see me in a month's time. I'll ponder over your case, and try to figure out what must be done about it. I'll tell you the day that you come back."

The houngan stood up.

"Oh, there's one more thing, Rossini," Desilus murmured.

"What else is there, my son?"

"I've one more thing to tell you about. It has to do with Sinette, the servant of Mist' Dutilleul."

Desilus told the story of the young woman, adding all manner of details, including the incident of the black butterfly and the broken mirror, the cutting down of the mapou tree, the drunkenness of Morin the very night of the sacrilege and a quantity of other more or less absurd incidents. Few of them seemed to have any bearing on the heart of the problem, which was to bring Morin back to the arms of Sinette. But Rossini quickly understood what he was talking about, and sniffing a nice, fat offering, promised to fix up everything.

"You must bring Sinette with you when you return," he said as he opened the door to show his visitor out.

"That's fine, Rossini," said Desilus. "And how much will it cost to fix up my business?"

"Don't bother your head about that. For you it will be next to nothing."

Desilus thanked him effusively and took leave of the houngan.

As he went down the road he looked back to see if this time, by some miracle, pigeons might not fly out of the windows of the house. That would surely be a good sign for him, little pigeons strutting in their parade of love, bowing and scraping to each other. But once more his hopes were dashed. He drew some comfort from his session with the houngan, however, and was convinced that the voodoo priest would finally deprive his son of this diabolic power of a werewolf with which he was endowed. So he decided to stop at Madan Horace's for a quick drink. He walked along briskly, humming a bawdy song from the Rara country festivals, in which a young girl from the region, who has been left pregnant by some unknown lover, is taunted in fairly crude terms:

> Grosse, oh! grosse, oh! grosse, oh!
> Arelise, grosse, oh!
> Grosse, oh! Arelise, grosse, oh!

Bossuet disappeared soon after the incident of the mapou tree. He left the region in such a strange manner that it was clear to everyone that he was about to draw down an implacable vengeance for the harm caused him by Morin Dutilleul.

One afternoon, possessed by some strange spirit unknown to the people of Musseau, he dashed into Horace's yard, dressed in the red garb of a general, with horns on his head and dragging behind him a big clanking chain tied around his waist. In this strange getup he pranced and snorted about the yard like a horse. At the sight of this terrifying apparition, the big shopkeeper fainted in her armchair behind the counter.

Horace, thinking it was the devil himself who had possessed his brother-in-law and was "riding him", ran to his room and grabbed a crucifix and a bottle of holy water. Immediately Bossuet, or rather the spirit who possessed him, uttered cries of rage and foamed at the mouth like a mad dog.

"Vade retro Satanus," solemnly chanted the carpenter in stilted pig-Latin.

The "thing" drew back in terror. With great agile leaps and bounds it dodged the sprinklings of holy water and the motions of the cross that Horace made in its direction. When chased from the porch it tried to enter the house through another door. But the carpenter, protected by his Christian faith, pursued it so cleverly and so well that it fled from the vicinity of the store howling with raucous cries.

From that day on nobody had seen Bossuet in the region, and naturally many comments on what might happen next were the principal subject of all conversations. Madan Horace was convinced that he had fled to the Forban Grotto. But what she could not understand, and this worried her considerably, was why the spirit who had "ridden" her brother had first led him to her house. That could only portend some calamity. But the carpenter was convinced, and he never tired of repeating it to his wife, that he had mastered the devil and consequently there was nothing more to fear from him. Furthermore, should the "thing" make its appearance again, he need only face it as he had the first time to drive it off again. In case that didn't work, he could still call upon Father Eusebius for help, and in a twinkling the priest would exorcise the evil one.

However firm his own conviction, still he did not succeed in dissipating the fears of Madan Horace. The poor woman's nights were haunted by the most absurd and frightful nightmares. They disturbed her so much that she began to have hallucinations.

She would awake with a nervous start and say that she heard the sound of chains and pots being dragged through the courtyard. Sometimes she heard the mooing of a cow, or the grunting of a pig, or again the prancing of a multitude of donkeys, dancing in the moonlight. Horace would get up, open the door an inch or two to peek out, and assure her he could see none of the things she said she heard. But one morning, about four o'clock, as she was going out to prepare the coffee, she uttered a shrill scream of horror and remained rooted to the spot, shaking in all her limbs. The carpenter rushed to her aid. She stretched out a trembling hand.

"There, Horace, there! Look! Don't you see them going down the main road?"

"Now what do you see?" her husband asked, trying to appear cool.

"The donkeys and the ox, driven by the pig!" she moaned. "There, look well! Don't you see them?"

"No, I don't see anything," he said, but he was shivering. "And I don't want to see them!"

His hair stood on end. He made the sign of the cross, dragged his wife back into the house, and slammed and bolted the door. . . .

When Desilus reached the general store, Madan Horace was telling the sheriff about her latest dream. Charles and the carpenter listened meditatively as they smoked their short pipes, both agitated, but each for a different reason.

"She was an old, wizened Negress, I tell you, Sheriff,"

Madan Horace said, full of a tense excitement. "She stood there at the foot of my bed, dressed entirely in black. She looked at me a long time like that, nodding her head, her chin resting on one hand, but not budging from the spot. Finally she talked to me: 'Elise, my child, someone is trying to harm you. They would like to devour the child you carry in your womb.' Then, smiling sadly, she added: 'And it's a member of your own family, yes, who is plotting to do that'."

"Oh my, my, my!" the justice of the peace clucked. "There are indeed some people who have a curse on them!"

Desilus was moved by what she had said.

"And she didn't tell you who it was who was trying to harm you?" he asked innocently.

"Who should know?" Ti-Charles sniggered. "But my poor Desilus, we don't really have to name him for you to know who it is, do we?"

Understanding that the young man referred to Bossuet, Madan Horace silenced him with an irritated glance, and continued her account.

"Then the woman spoke to me again: 'You are my child. I will not let them do that to you. Tomorrow morning, before speaking to anyone, you must take two leaves of jockey club, three leaves of basil, and a handful of rice and sprinkle them in your bath.' Then the woman disappeared. . . ."

"Now I understand," said the justice of the peace. "That old Negress was one of your early ancestors who is watching over you. That explains it!"

Horace disdainfully shrugged his shoulders.

"How could you know that, Delisca? Did she tell you

too? As for me, I know that the devil always appears in such shapes to lead us into sin. It couldn't be the Holy Virgin, nor the saints, nor any of the dead. What's more, no follower of the Good Lord ever makes use of medicinal herbs."

"So, Horace, you believe that medicinal herbs are evil too?"

"Yes, Sheriff, that's what I believe. And Father Eusebius also believes it. And that is why I prevented Madan Horace from taking such a bath. It was the devil himself who recommended it to her."

Delisca was overwhelmed with dismay.

"You didn't do that, did you, Horace? You dared to do that? Very well then, papa, I'll give you no more of my advice. But remember, when calamity strikes in your own house, that you will have no reason to lament. You will know then what brought it down upon you and that you yourself asked for it."

He got up briskly to leave.

"If it's a matter of driving the devil out of my house," boasted Horace in a stubborn and conceited tone, "I know how to do that. It is within the power of each one of us. I've done it before."

traight and silent in her blue cotton print dress, an orange madras bound about her head, Irma left her parents' cabin where she had just made herself ready for her lover's visit.

The day declined softly. The olive-drab foliage, tinted violet for a moment in the pools of shadow, faded and became blurred into the deepening blackness. But the sky, where stars already began to glow, still dragged the pale green iridescent fringe of her robe across the slopes of the hills to the east.

The young girl went to seat herself on a big flat stone at the entrance of the courtyard like a squatting washerwoman, her legs spread wide, her skirt tucked between her thighs. Thus she awaited her fiance each evening—motionless, her gaze fixed and distant, sinking down into a profound, dreamlike reverie.

From time to time she would sigh to herself. Or a few words would escape from her moving lips.

"Little kitten!" she would murmur. Or simply, "Beloved of my heart."

Then the lines of her mouth would grow rigid and she would relapse into silence. It was a sort of incantation to hasten the arrival of the young man, and also an internal chant extolling him. She did these things mechanically, unaware of herself, thinking entirely of him. . . .

Ti-Charles, what a brave fellow he was! A real man in every way. . . .

Of course some people said he chased after the women; but was it his fault if at his slightest gesture they would throw themselves into his arms? Doesn't the proverb say that a good cock sings in all the chicken coops? The essential fact for Irma was that after these furtive liaisons her lover always returned completely to her, like an earthenware jug that one offers to any passerby who begs for a drink, but which he will not fail to give back as soon as his thirst is quenched. And so the girl shrugged disdainfully at gossipers.

Moreover, Ti-Charles did not conduct himself with her as do some suitors who drag things out, planning to celebrate Easter before fasting through Lent, and then slip away once their desire has been satisfied. Far from acting in this way, he had proposed to marry her right away; but Alcaeus, Irma's father, finding them too young to set up house, had postponed the marriage to the following year, around Christmas time.

This delay seemed interminable to the young woman. She must patiently wait eight long months more, and they already had waited so long! Irma would grind her teeth just thinking about it, and was irritated with her father, whose reasons she could not understand. She would willingly have dispensed with Alcaeus's consent and gone to live under the same roof with her lover, while awaiting the blessing of marriage, were it not for the respect she owed her father. And of course Ti-Charles would surely have judged such parental disrespect very improper. At least that is what she would say to herself to calm her fits of anger.

She was thus expressing only a feeble whim. At heart she was a fatalist and quickly submitted to the laws of fate. Apart from these twinges of revolt, she never impatiently desired anything which could not be achieved immediately. And so she was really content with Ti-Charles' regular visits and his chaste caresses. Whenever he took her in his arms, she would turn her thoughts back to the past, trying to live again the unforgettable instant when, matured by an exalting rapture, they had promised themselves to each other, and would thereby stifle her imperious desire for sexual contact.

What a surprise it had been for her! Having the same godfather as herself, Charles was, as they say, her baptismal brother. They had played together as little children, growing up side by side, and until they reached the age of puberty would go swimming naked in the spring along with all the other children of Musseau. After that, being her elder by three years, he had always treated her as a young girl. How could she have guessed that one fine day he would really fall in love with her?

It had happened all of a sudden the year before, at the Rara country festival during Holy Week. Aroused to a pitch of nervous excitement by the bamboo trumpets and the rhythm of a warrior's march which, at regular intervals, was punctuated by the low bellow of shining lambis sea-conch shells, the strident notes of whistles and the crack of whips through four whole days and nights, the young people of Musseau wandered through the entire countryside together. They completed a wide circuit and joined in the festivities at Bourdon and all the other villages of the area. At each place they visited they were wined and dined. They sang and danced . . . danced . . . danced . . .

> "You've put our home too close to papa!
> You've built our cabin too near mama!
> Each time I wriggle papa hears me, oh! oh!
> And mama hears each sigh of love, oh! oh!"

That and a score of other folksongs they sang as they danced.

The dawn of Easter Monday broke fresh and clear, and all the countryside still vibrated with the Dionysian tumult of this springtime festival. The voices of the women, sharp and incisive as the first rays of the rising sun, pierced the deep chorus of male voices and rose high into the sky.

> "Calypso, you are a woman just like me;
> To you I tell what Sonson did to me.
> I caressed Sonson,
> I fondled Sonson,
> I even went so far I nibbled Sonson!
> When I begged Sonson something in return,
> Sonson only snored the louder,
> Sonson, he would not arise! . . ."

Irma's voice was the highest pitched, the most ardent. Giving her the cue, Ti-Charles for the first time looked at her as one will look at a woman he desires. His eyes were set and burning, but without the slightest sign of impertinence.

"You've put our home too close to papa!
You've built our cabin too near mama!
Each time I wriggle papa hears me, oh! oh!
And mama hears each sigh of love, oh! oh!"

When morning came they found themselves somehow
alone on the road back to her home. They were troubled
and silent, but inside themselves the sweetest and most intimate bonds were forged. Bidding her good-bye at the gate
to her home, Ti-Charles looked away, and then said in a
firm voice:

"Tomorrow I will write your father and mother. . . ."
She turned, and running like a woman possessed, rushed
into the house, her heart pounding.

The letter had been drafted by Horace and he had re-
copied it in his most beautiful handwriting. The thick and
thin strokes of the pen were traced with painstaking sym-
metry, on special paper with a border of fine, gilded imita-
tion lacework and a letterhead decorated with a basket of
blue forget-me-nots and two blue swallows. The contents
of the letter were simple and unaffected:

Musseau, This 10 April 1936
To:
Master and Dame Alcaeus Jean-Baptiste and
Marie-Noel Dorleans.
Master and Dame,

*I take up my pen in writing you this letter of request to
ask you for the hand of your dear young daughter Irma
whom I desire to take as my wife.*

*I trust this will meet with your most agreeable and wel-
come consent.*

Please accept, Sir and Madam, my most distinguished
salutations.

Signed:
Charles Metelus.

This letter had been solemnly delivered to the parents
of the young woman by Horace. They were surprised and
shocked by this request for their daughter's hand. They
thought that Irma and Ti-Charles, having been held over
the baptismal font by the same godfather, were obliged to
consider themselves, before God and man, as brother and
sister. Their marriage would therefore be nothing less than
incest. Peasant customs had always decreed matters this
way. But Horace, who was free of these superstitious beliefs, assured them that neither the Catholic religion nor
the law agreed with them on this point. Nevertheless, they
would not believe him.

"Irma is Ti-Charles' sister," Alcaeus repeated. "Therefore they cannot be married."

Horace was forced to bring them to Father Eusebius in
order to convince them. The priest finally overcame their
reluctance. . . .

Although she found it a delightful pastime to let these
memories come to her mind again (or perhaps because it
was so sweet) Irma felt that Ti-Charles was late in coming.
Her impatience gradually increased to the point of real
irritation. And, as though to displease her even more, he
arrived very late that evening.

"What do you mean," she remarked dryly, "arriving
at this hour of the night?"

"But it wasn't my fault," the young man replied, sitting

on the ground close beside her. "Just as I was about to go out, a friend came to see me. It was Desilus himself."

"Couldn't you excuse yourself?"

"I really couldn't, dearest. He had to talk to me about a very serious matter."

"Ah, yes indeed, I understand," she retorted in a voice which hissed with rage. "Coming to see me isn't a serious matter at all, is it? It's only for your own amusement!"

Ti-Charles suppressed an angry retort.

"Irma! What you're saying isn't fair. And you know it very well!"

"How should I know if this friend of whom you speak wasn't a woman, one of those numerous young things who are always chasing around after you?"

Charles jumped up, furious. For once, indeed, his conscience was really clear! Something had already happened to irritate him, and now he let himself go!

"Since that's the way you feel about it," he said, "I think there's no further reason for me to come to visit you."

He pretended to be leaving. But, instantly alarmed, Irma held him back by the arm.

"What makes you so angry? Don't you see that I simply wanted to chide you a little for being late?"

She pleaded with him, trying to force a smile. Charles continued to sulk.

"Well, if that's the way you judge me . . ."

"Who says that I'm trying to judge you? . . . Come now, Ti-Charles, can't anyone joke with you any more?"

"Sure, Irma, sure they can. Especially you. But please understand, dearest, that it isn't good to say all the words that rise to your lips. Some of them can hurt. You can try hard to take them back afterwards, but the harm they've done remains. And that's why old people used to say that begging pardon does not heal wounds."

"So, dear, you are really angry with me?"

"No, Irma. You know very well that isn't possible . . ."

It was their very first quarrel. Seeing that it had now been dispelled, Irma tenderly and impulsively squeezed the hand of her fiancé, as young girls often do.

"Hush, Ti-Charles!" she whispered. "Let's forget such petty things. Sit down here beside me and tell me what your friend came to tell you. That must really have been serious, for you to keep me waiting."

"Yes, Irma, it was serious . . . It was very, very serious . . ."

He paused for a moment.

"It had to do with Bossuet. . . . Do you recall that horrible 'thing' he goes to visit in the Forban Gorge from time to time?"

"The Cigouave?" Irma asked, a strange uneasiness gripping her.

"Well, it was about the Cigouave, Irma . . . Desilus came to tell me that last night he heard the beast howling in Master Morin's courtyard."

"He heard it!" the girl groaned.

"Yes, he heard it. But that isn't all. Desilus, wanting to find out what was going on, got up without making a sound, opened the door a tiny crack, and there he saw the 'thing' which was leaping high in the air, turning somersaults, like a little kid. . . ."

"No, no, Ti-Charles! Enough!" she begged, closing her eyes with fear and leaning against him. "Enough, enough!"

"But what frightens you, Irma?" the young man asked.

"The 'thing' certainly hasn't come for us. It has come for Master Morin."

"Yes, Ti-Charles, I know very well that it's after him. But wasn't it Bossuet who sent the Cigouave here? Then who knows for certain that it is only Master Morin that he is after? Hasn't he also got it in for you?"

The young man did not answer, even though the same foreboding had already crossed his mind. He got up to say goodnight.

"But you're not leaving already?" she said, a note of reproach in her voice.

"Yes, I'm going," he said.

He didn't want to add, for fear of upsetting her, that if he wished to return at this early hour it was to avoid the risk of meeting the Cigouave, which might happen if he lingered. She also felt this and did not try to hold him back, as she might have done under other conditions. But she insisted on walking part of the way with him. As they were in their last embrace before separating she suddenly felt an overwhelming need to give herself to him. It was not so much physical desire that drove her to it, but an obscure foreboding that perhaps never again would it be possible.

"Take me, Ti-Charles, take me!" she panted, her warm breath on his face, as she gripped him tightly around the neck and tried to draw him down to the earth.

Charles resisted and tried to break loose from her clinging arms. She arched her back, pressed her belly and thighs tightly against his body, pulling him down with all her strength. Her breath came in sharp, staccato gasps and her body quivered in every muscle. He soon gave in. His body followed hers softly down to the earth, and silently, without a cry, they merged their bodies until they were one.

orin Dutilleul was comfortably installed on a couch, cooling himself on the veranda after the sweltering heat of the day. The moon had just risen and bathed the sleeping trees with a thick, shadowless light. A soft breeze touched them with its faint breath from time to time, scarcely ruffling the limp, drooping foliage. The calm of this luxuriant landscape, where nature gorgeously displayed her splendors, aroused romantic dreams in him. But its peaceful silence seemed so pure that Morin felt that even his innermost thoughts were an indiscretion in the midst of it. And he was in no mood to dream that night, or any other night for that matter.

If only for an instant he could stifle the tumult of anguish and anger which agitated him! On certain evenings he was tormented even in his sleep, which alcohol often peopled with the contorted shapes of nightmares. He was no longer capable of resisting the overwhelming desire to drink whenever this anguish gripped him. Everything, moreover, contributed to maintain him in this morbid state; particularly the yearning for his dead wife which was nourished by his realizing how false were his illusions of country life, the hostility of the peasants of Musseau towards him, their terrible secret practice of sorcery, and above all, the fear that one day they would succeed in winning over his own household servants to their cause.

For several days past the attitude of his servants puzzled

and worried him. Not only had their work become slip-shod, but Morin frequently would surprise them in mysterious discussions, and their agitated faces betrayed the profound anxiety which gripped them. The instant they saw him coming they hastened, abashed, to separate and go about their separate tasks. He had fruitlessly tried to question them discreetly, hoping to win their confidence. But he only extracted confused and stammering responses from them, in which he found not the slightest hint of the real cause of their unusual conduct.

Some foul deed was surely being plotted against him, thought Morin Dutilleul, and he had no doubt that Bossuet was at the heart of it. His dramatic disappearance from the region, which always preceded his evil revenges, was enough to put any man who was not his friend on guard.

Morin had reached this point in his reflections when he heard three sharp blasts of a whistle, followed by the terrible howling of some beast. Then a man screamed pathetically for help. Something horrible was going on down by the spring.

"Help! Help! . . . Desilus! . . . Help! The beast has been set upon me!"

Again Morin heard the sharp blasts of the whistle. A howl answered it. This was repeated several times and then suddenly all was still again. Morin excitedly grabbed his revolver, which he only removed from the holster on his belt when he was going to bed at night. He shouted for his hired man, but Desilus, shivering with fear on his mat, was careful not to betray his presence by answering. But even had he wished to answer, his throat was so constricted by fear that he could not utter the slightest sound. Nevertheless, when Morin, unnerved, came hammering on his door he found sufficient strength to rise and open it, and giving way to habit, obeyed the orders of his master and followed him out into the night without fretting.

When they reached the spring they saw the body of a man stretched on the other bank of the torrent, bathed in the moonlight. He lay in a heap, inert as a corpse. Desilus shivered.

"Mist' Dutilleul," he pleaded in a choking voice. "I beg you, go no further. This is something that doesn't concern us in the least."

Morin hesitated despite himself, and the fear of his hired man communicated itself to him. In fact, why did he let himself be involved in this affair? What did he have in common with the natives of this place, who despised him? But that was only his first reaction, and he quickly recovered. His human sentiments gained the upper hand over his fear and rancor, for he had conserved these qualities despite everything.

"That's enough of your stupidity," he snapped at the hired man. "Come on, let's see what has happened to the poor fellow."

As they drew near the body Desilus uttered a cry of anguish, for he recognized that it was Ti-Charles. Morin bent over, and placed his hand on the young man's breast. He was still breathing, but he was a pitiful sight to see. His disordered clothing had been torn as if by some giant claws, the crotch of his trousers was soaked with blood, and a look of extreme horror was frozen on his face from some terrible thing he had seen as he fainted. Morin turned towards Desilus.

"Come here and help me. We'll carry him up to the house."

"Oh, Mist' Dutilleul!" the hired man protested. "What can you be saying? Don't you think it would be better to call the neighbors to our assistance?"

"But nobody would come, imbecile! In this cursed village all men are like you, they have a deadly fear of the spirits. They wouldn't dare come to help us. The best thing to do is to carry this poor boy back to the house, where we can revive him and bind up his wounds."

"No, Mist' Dutilleul, we can't do that," Desilus insisted. "Please, Master, just for once take my advice! I am from these parts. I know what this means. If I beg you not to get yourself mixed up in this affair, I have good reasons. My father used to quote me an old saying: 'A fish lives in the water. If one should announce to you that the crocodile is sick, believe him.' Mist' Dutilleul, the justice of the peace doesn't live far from here. Let me call him and he'll come. It's his duty to do so."

The hired man cupped his hands and without waiting for Morin's permission, shouted at the top of his lungs.

"Houe! . . . Houe! . . . Delisca! . . . Hou-hou! . . . Delisca, oh! . . . This is Desilus calling. This is me . . ."

The justice of the peace immediately answered him, as if he had been alert and waiting for some such call.

"Houe! . . . Desilus! . . . Houe! . . . What has happened?"

"Charles has been hurt! . . . Hurry! . . . Come at once! . . . Down by the spring!"

"Charles has been hurt? . . . Oh! Oh! . . . Wait for me. . . . I'm coming."

He arrived, escorted by his adjutant Polycarp, and both

of his sons, who lighted the way for their father with blazing pine-knot torches. Suddenly noticing Morin in the shadows, the justice of the peace halted, intimidated.

"Oh, good evening, Master. . . . So you are also here!"

"Good evening, Sheriff," Morin replied. "Come close here with your light, so I can see where the boy is hurt."

Morin unbuttoned Ti-Charles' pants. He immediately uttered a cry of horror. The young man's genital organs had been lacerated into an indistinguishable pulp. There was every indication that he had been attacked by a dog, the mark of fangs was recognizable at first glance. Morin stood up, turned his eyes away from the disgusting sight, which made him sick to his stomach.

"Only the Cigouave could have done that!" whispered the hired man, awed. "I knew it was the Cigouave when it howled just before attacking him. . . ."

"The Cigouave? It sounded just like a mad dog to me," Morin sarcastically corrected him. "Instead of imagining such silly things, come with me to the house. I'm going to fetch some rum and try to bring the poor fellow back to his senses. Meanwhile these gentlemen will guard him. Won't you, Sheriff Delice?"

The justice of the peace didn't share his views. He thought the best thing would be to carry the young man immediately to his sister's home where, he explained, it would be easier to bind up his wounds as soon as he had been revived. Morin rubbed his hands to show that he washed his hands of the whole business.

"As you wish, Sheriff! I don't want to be more royalist than the king."

And, followed by his hired man, he marched off to the house, not at all displeased, moreover, to get away from this sad spectacle which was much too painful for his bourgeois sensibilities.

When they reached the house Desilus bade him good night. But to the great astonishment of the hired man Morin invited him in for a shot of rum to regain their composure. Following the custom of the country, the master ordered his servant to go and fetch his own glass.

Desilus needed no urging to bring it. He needed a stiff drink. Morin poured him three fingers of Barbancourt, which he put down in one gulp, after sprinkling the ground with a few drops to quench the thirst of the dead.

"Ah!" he clicked his tongue politely to show his pleasure. "How very good it is, Mist' Dutilleul!"

Morin poured him another. His real aim was to be agreeable to Desilus, in the hope that once the alcohol had loosened his tongue he could start chatting with his hired man, who might finally decide to speak frankly. Although he felt he knew the rational explanation for the misfortune which had befallen Ti-Charles, it nevertheless seemed very strange to him. For even if it had only been a dog which had attacked and bitten the young man, as was clearly the case, (the mark of its teeth was proof enough) what could be the meaning of the whistle blasts which accompanied the howling fury of the beast? What else could it mean, except that some person had guided him to his prey by means of the whistle?

"Well, what do you think, Desilus?" Morin asked him outright, after a few drinks. "In your opinion could it only have been the Cigouave which lacerated Ti-Charles in his private parts?"

"Yes, sir, Mist' Dutilleul. There can be no doubt of it. It was the beast which attacked him."

"Very well then. But surely some person sent it to this very spot?"

"Most certainly. The Cigouave never comes on its own account."

Morin looked his hired man straight in the eye.

"And so it must have been Bossuet who led it here to Musseau?"

Desilus nodded his head, chattering nervously.

"Excuse me, Mist' Dutilleul, but don't you understand it's never good to talk about these things, especially at night?"

He stood up and prepared to leave. Prudently he asked: "Master, don't you think it must be rather late? Wouldn't it be better for us to go to bed?"

And Morin, understanding that he would get nothing more out of him, bade him good night, although he showed his displeasure at being forced to do so. He reproached him for his stupidity and cowardice, which were only too obvious. But Desilus had long since accustomed himself to the rude remarks of his master.

Ti-Charles finally regained consciousness in Horace's house where he had been carried and treated. He wept at the loss of his virility, for he was convinced that the Cigouave's fangs had rendered him impotent, although everyone in the house assured him that his wounds didn't seem to be "as bad as that."

Madan Horace came in to sit by his sickbed, and softly caressed his head.

"Are you in much pain, little brother?" she asked with deep maternal tenderness.

And when he remained silent, she added: "Tell me how you feel, please."

"How I feel? Madan Horace! . . ." he smiled wryly. Then his face grew sad.

"How I feel doesn't matter now, not in the condition I'm in!" His voice was bitter. "Only one thing matters now, revenge! I must find Bossuet and strangle him before I die. He's the one who sent this calamity upon me!"

"Bossuet!" moaned the shopkeeper.

"When I tried to tell you that he could only harm the poor black Negroes of the countryside, you wouldn't believe me. Now you see how he avoided touching Master Morin to turn against me. And I never did him any harm, never!"

He began to sob again, but this time he strangled from impotent rage.

"Well, Sheriff," asked Horace, "will you advise the city officials tomorrow to send us an ambulance from the hospital?"

Ti-Charles protested energetically.

"Now," he observed, "only the spirits can decide whether I can be saved or not. You and your doctors! They would be worse than useless in an affair of this kind. They only know how to treat people who are sick from natural causes . . . and even then, you never know! Keep your doctors away from me!"

"They don't only have doctors at the hospital," retorted the carpenter. "They also have priests and nuns there. They also have the chapel, not to mention the grotto of Notre Dame de Lourdes in the park where miracles are performed every day."

Madan was not of the same opinion as her husband. She

felt that the best thing they could do in the circumstances would be to call in the voodoo priest Rossini, for now only the spirits could perform a miracle for her brother.

"Listen here, woman!" her husband shouted at her in a stern, sharp-pitched voice. "Did I ask you for your opinion?"

Then, turning to the justice of the peace, he ordered:

"So then, Sheriff, it's understood! You will take the necessary steps to transport my brother-in-law Ti-Charles to the hospital tomorrow!"

Delisca ponderously shook his head, as if to lend more weight to what he was about to say. He removed his colonial helmet and swabbed his forehead, which was beaded with sweat.

"If it were a matter of remaining within the law," he finally declared, "then what Boss Horace asks me to do would be the course to follow. The law says that whenever one man is wounded by another, I must notify the authorities in town. And after I have advised them it is up to them to have him brought to the hospital. That, my friends, is the law—"

"So now you see," the carpenter turned triumphantly to his wife, "when I say something I know what I'm talking about. I'm not a child, not me!"

"But then, on the other hand," the justice of the peace went on, as if he had never been interrupted, "there is also the fact that we are many poor Negroes in this land of Haiti. And we know that there are certain things that the official laws do not cover. . . . It was the rich people in the city, not us, who made that kind of law to regulate their own affairs. And everybody knows that they haven't the slightest idea of what is good for our people . . . and that's also why I don't think the doctors at the hospital can do anything to heal Ti-Charles' wounds. Godfather Horace, I also believe that instead of notifying them we should call on Rossini to help him. Only if Rossini is able to reach some agreement with the spirits will there be any chance of saving your brother-in-law. If he doesn't succeed, my friends, then ai-ai-ai! . . . It's just too bad—"

The carpenter indignantly broke in.

"Sheriff, the spirits of whom you speak are simply devils, the children of Lucifer! If the Lord is with you, they can do you no harm."

"Now, now, don't misunderstand me!" the justice of the peace started in again. "I don't pretend for an instant that we must not serve the Good Lord, for I too am a Christian. But I also believe, devils or not, that it is not good for us to turn our backs on the tribal Gods of Guinea, whom our ancestors passed on from father to son all the way down to us . . ."

This violent argument between Horace and Sheriff Delice raged on late into the night. In the end all those present were of the opinion that the latter had proved his point, and it was decided that they should call on the science of Rossini to try to save Ti-Charles. At this point the carpenter fell into a rage.

"If that's the way it's to be," he announced pontifically, "then I will not let Charles remain in my home! He must return to his own house by tomorrow morning. I refuse to permit the devil to set foot in this house!"

And so it was agreed, to the satisfaction of everyone.

The shopkeeper greeted Houngan Rossini and escorted him to the little hut where Ti-Charles lay on his sickbed. As he was about to cross the threshold he seemed to run up against some invisible obstacle—a magic circle or a hostile spirit who intended to bar his way into the hut.

"Oh-ho! What's this!" Rossini exclaimed, straightening up.

Then, stamping his foot petulantly on the ground and pacing to and fro before the door, he challenged the invisible spirit.

"Try your tricks on others!" he cried. "Hang it, can't you see that I'm not a stupid macaco monkey? You can't stump me with silly little tricks like that!"

So saying, he drew a large red bandana from his pocket, waved it in the air before him, wiped his face and then knotted it around his neck. This rite completed, he entered the cabin bearing his head proud and high, to the great admiration of Madan Horace, who already believed, without this further demonstration, that he was gifted with great powers over things and people.

The room was crudely furnished. In addition to the pallet there was only one white-pine chair and a filthy table on which were scattered a white enamel cup, a chipped plate and an earthen jug. Rossini, who had been counting on a lucrative fee, felt his professional ardor sink as he glanced around the room. But at that very instant, as though he guessed the houngan's deception, Ti-Charles uttered a loud groan. Whereupon the shopkeeper, moved by her young brother's lament, joined her hands pleadingly:

"Save him for me, Rossini! Save him! . . . I'll give you anything you want . . . Only save him!"

And Rossini, knowing that she was well off, hastened to reassure her.

"Don't worry any longer, Madan Horace. He is now in my hands, and I promise to treat him with all the devotion I would give to my own son."

Then he sat down in the chair beside the young man's bed and questioned him on the details of his accident. Ti-Charles' face muscles contracted, as though he were making a superhuman effort to stifle the pain which gripped him.

"I was on my way home from Irma's house. She had accompanied me part of the way," he began. Then he faltered, overcome by a sudden fit of sobbing at the memory of those sweet moments they had passed together, and which could never again be theirs.

"Go on," the houngan prompted him. "A man must keep his courage to face life. Giving way to tears as you are doing will get you nowhere."

"Wait a moment, it will pass," the young man said. Then he went on. "You must understand, Rossini, none of this was my fault, not at all!"

He paused again to get a grip on himself, and explained to the houngan the dishonest proposals that Bossuet had made to his fiancée. Then he recalled the past visits of his brother to the Forban Gorge and his sudden disappearance after the chopping down of the mapou tree by the spring. He stressed this incident especially.

"It was at that very spot," he concluded, "that the Cigouave hurled itself upon me and ripped me . . . you know where!"

Rossini listened and nodded his head, full of unction and gravity.

"Ah, now I understand! This is not a small matter, indeed. That is a terrible 'thing' that someone has sent to attack you."

He heaved a deep sigh. Then, turning towards Madan Horace he asked: "Have you brought everything I need?"

"Yes," she replied. "I have brought everything. The olive oil is in the cup on the table before you."

She thrust her hand into the pocket of her ample dress, drew out two coins and a bit of cotton wool, which she held out to him.

"Here are the seven centimes and the cotton."

The houngan put the coins on the bare ground, placed the dish over them and poured the oil into it. Then, he prepared seven little wicks with the cotton wool, arranged them around the edge of the dish, and lit them. Having completed these preparations, he knelt beside the bed, raised his eyes to heaven and, bleating like a little goat, began a votive prayer.

"Saint Radegund, brave Baron Samedi, guardian of the cemeteries! Great saint, endowed with the power to traverse purgatory unharmed, preserve me from all evils, keep all my enemies fully occupied, so that they will leave me in peace. Jesus! Master of all things, living and dead, judge this cause for me and my children! Bring to naught all plots which have been hatched against them! Sanctify the converted Judges and the Sinners. Great Saint Radegund, deliver me from those who hate me! I pledge to offer in your name an Our Father and a Hail Mary. Beseech your soul that it may deliver me. All-Powerful God, who suffered death on the cross, particularly for our sins, have pity on me! Holy Cross of Jesus Christ, pour into my being all your goodness. Jesus of Nazareth, have pity on me! Cause all evil spirits to flee from me. Brave Baron Saturday, I deliver myself wholly into your hands. Dear Brave One, Amen!"

"Amen!" responded the shopkeeper.

The houngan blessed himself again.

"Now," he said, "the Good Lord is with us. And all the saints and angels of Paradise."

He stood up, took the dish and extended it to the four principal points of the compass. Then he dipped his thumb into the oil which he had just consecrated, and made the sign of the cross on Ti-Charles' wounds. He turned and spoke to the shopkeeper again.

"And where is the pigeon?" he asked in a dry and haughty voice.

"It's right here!" Madan Horace promptly replied.

She drew a wicker basket from under the bed, extracted the prescribed victim from it and held it out to the houngan. He immediately took the live bird, expertly broke its feet, its wings and finally its neck. After which, splitting open the body from top to bottom, he drew out the pigeon's viscera, still hot and smoking, and placed them on Ti-Charles' head. . . .

And that was all the treatment Charles received on this first visit!

That same day Morin Dutilleul vainly tried again to extract from his hired man some fact which might help him to find an accurate explanation for the catastrophe which had befallen Ti-Charles. But Desilus would parry every question put to him with some obscure native proverb or parable whose meaning escaped Morin. The old man seemed fantastic and absurd to him. He soon tired of questioning him, understanding full well that he was merely wasting his time.

He never doubted, of course, that Bossuet's brother had simply been lacerated by a common dog. But the circumstances under which the attack had occurred still left him confused and perplexed.

The blasts of the whistle to which the beast had responded with its howls surely indicated that someone accompanied and guided it. Unless . . . Morin Dutilleul started with fright and horror as the thought struck him. He recalled that in Africa it sometimes happened that a crafty malefactor would disguise himself as a panther to tear open his victim with metal claws, ripping and scratching in such a way that the wounds inflicted resembled those made by a real wild beast. It was very possible, he thought, that this criminal tradition might still be preserved among some of the peasants, slightly modified under the influence of former superstitious planters—and they had almost all been superstitious. The colonial planters must also have transmitted to their slaves their own belief in lycanthropy, for most peasants still believed that any man could be transformed into a werewolf, a wolf—or any other animal for that matter!

This hypothesis was perfectly feasible. But the mark of fangs which he had noticed on the genital organs of the young man invalidated it. So he was indeed obliged to return to his original theory of a dog whom someone had cleverly trained. It must surely have been a big and power-ful dog, since, according to Ti-Charles' account which had been relayed to Morin, the beast had bounded upon him and knocked him over with ease.

This left to clarify only the question of the point which the beast had chosen to attack. Yes, why, indeed, had it torn the young man's groin rather than some other part of his body? This did seem very strange, especially if one were to discard every explanation by supernatural causes. It really frightened Morin Dutilleul. And he shook his head in despair at these proofs of what a crafty and danger-ous man Bossuet really was. How quick-tempered and foolish he had been to provoke him!

There was another cardinal point that particularly wor-ried him. Why had his adversary turned the beast against Ti-Charles, who was his own brother and who had done nothing which might justify such a frightful aggression? There could be no doubt that the scoundrel coveted the young man's fiancée. But how could such a caprice in an inveterate woman chaser—for it surely could not be real passion which moved him—become so strong that it would drive him to commit such a horrible crime? The man was cruel, that was clear. And he was without any scruples whatever when he set out to reach some goal. Another idea flashed into Morin's mind. Perhaps . . . perhaps, by acting in this way he had really intended to give his sworn en-emy, Morin himself, some idea of the terrible fate that was reserved for him if he did not get out of the district at once. . . . Suppose that were the real motive behind this first crime!

All day long the people of Musseau flocked to the cabin to learn how Ti-Charles was getting on. Madan Horace received them at the door, which she barred with the imposing mass of her body, and patiently answered all their questions. Some of them, either more deeply touched by the suffering of their friend, or simply urged on by boundless curiosity, expressed a desire to go in to see him. But the shopkeeper parried their requests by saying that her brother was resting and that the houngan who was treating him had recommended that he should not be tired out by any visits. They went away without insisting, promising, however, to return the next day. . . .

Since Rossini's departure, Ti-Charles moaned no more. A burning fever had plunged him into an extreme state of dejection bordering on stupor. His suffering had not benumbed his whole body, but although the pain had spread throughout his abdomen and crotch, it no longer tormented him with the burning spasms that at first seemed to pierce to every part of his body. And the spring flies buzzing around him gave him the painful impression of being suspended in infinite space. They buzzed and turned and turned and turned!

The low murmur of conversations at the door, and all the peaceful sounds of the countryside, the crowing of a cock, the mooing of a cow, the shrill voice of a child, the haunting song of the washerwomen, drifted in to him as from a distant world. From time to time the image of Irma would begin to form nebulously in his mind, then it would blur and quickly fade away. Finally he opened his haggard eyes, but closed them immediately, for the feeble light filtering into the cabin was like a sharp blow between his eyes.

Only the arrival of his father-in-law at last was able to drag him out of this morbid torpor.

"Charles, my son, what is this terrible calamity that

has fallen upon you?" Alcaeus asked him as he sat down on the chair. "Is what I have heard true, that the Cigouave has devoured your private parts?"

"Yes, it is true. Bossuet did this to me . . . He wants to abduct Irma as his mistress."

"Bossuet? What can you be saying? Why, isn't he your elder brother?"

"Ho-ho! Alcaeus, you don't mean to tell me you don't know about him yet? You could be his father, his mother or his wife, you could even be his own child, for all that matters. But if he desired something and you stood in his way, there is nothing he would not do to get rid of you. What difference is it to him that I should be his brother? Have you simply forgotten what he did some time ago to Ferdinand?"

Alcaeus fell silent, embarrassed. He knew very well that Ti-Charles was right. But peasant courtesy, made up in equal parts of involved scruples and discretion, forbade him to agree with the young man.

"Irma wanted to come here with me," he finally said, changing the subject. "But I wouldn't let her come. You know how women are . . . Ever since this morning she has done nothing but sit and cry!"

"You don't mean it!" the young man exclaimed.

Then, gripped by a sudden dread: "Does she know?" he asked with fear and shame.

"Oh, no, no! Nobody has dared to tell her about it. She only knows that the 'thing' attacked you and bit you. At what point? She hasn't asked, and it has not even been necessary to lie to her."

Charles breathed more easily. He took Alcaeus' hand in his, and squeezed it gratefully.

"Thanks, Alcaeus! Thank you! You're a real father-in-law, a really fine one!" the young man said earnestly, shedding tears of thanks. . . .

Night came with its procession of anguish and terror. Despite the heat, which had begun very early this year, everyone withdrew into their cabins early, barricaded their doors, and went to bed. But nobody could sleep. Their ears listening alertly, their hearts beating nervously, everyone waited.

The silence swelled with this unanimous tension, and it was not Morin Dutilleul alone who was oppressed by it. However, unlike the others, it was not fear that gripped him. He still would not admit to himself that the Cigouave was a supernatural being. He was becoming more and more convinced that someone was abusing the credulity of the peasants of Musseau, and that the Cigouave was in reality only a dog. And so, like all the others, he waited with bated breath. But unlike them he wanted to see the animal which terrorized the entire region, and so he sat glued by the window. He had armed himself with his pistol in preparation for the encounter and fortified his courage by drinking copiously all evening long.

Under the light of a full moon he watched the thickets in the vicinity of the spring, hoping to see the beast burst out of them at any moment. But it did not come until midnight, at a time when sleep, with the aid of alcohol, began to weigh heavily on his eyes. At first he did not see it. He heard it howl several times, in answer to the whistle blasts from its master. Then he heard the shrill squealing of a pig being butchered. The pig's horrible screams grew weaker and weaker until he could only hear the feeble grunts that marked the poor animal's death rattle. Then silence fell again, more dismal than before.

But soon, in the heavy shadows of a mango tree, a dim form appeared, flashing its phosphorescent eyes toward him. It was the beast. Hastily Morin grabbed his revolver and fired at it. The beast did not budge, and its eyes continued to gleam up at him. He took careful aim at them and fired a second time, but without greater success. He heard a voice laughing hollowly somewhere out there in the night and then the blast of a whistle. The beast uttered one last long howl and in a single bound plunged back into the deep shadows around the spring.

Morin's hair stood on end. The sweat of fear oozed from his pores, his teeth chattered and he trembled in every limb. With a great effort he drew back from the window. He walked with difficulty, his feet seemed to stick to the floor, and dropped heavily on the bed.

He did not succeed in regaining control of himself until much later. When he did he took a glass, filled it unsteadily with rum and tried to swallow it down. But so short and hard had his breathing become that he was able to gulp it only in small dribblets. Then he put out the light and went to bed. Everything began to spin around him. His feet rose slowly to the ceiling, then his head followed them. His suspended body rocked crazily from side to side, as if he were in some gigantic cradle. Finally he twisted himself into a knot, like a tourniquet. A cold draft, like a wind from the sea, bathed his face with raindrops.

And then the beast reappeared. It stood there, in his own room, and exactly as Desilus had described it, with the body of a dog, the head and feet of a man. Its eyes glowed intensely like a charcoal brazier, fire shot from its mouth. It sat on its haunches looking silently upon Morin, immobile, a sarcastic grin on its face. He awoke with a start. The beast was still there. Now it was crouching, creeping towards him, step by step. Aroused by terror, Morin screamed, jumped to the foot of the bed and tried to flee to the staircase. But the beast was there before him, standing at the doorway into the room. Then he rushed to the window, but the beast again barred his way. Saliva dripped from its strong jaws. And so, every way he turned to try to flee from the room, he found the Cigouave blocking his way. It began to chase him now. He broke into a run, dodging this way and that. He entangled himself in a chair in his precipitous flight and sprawled headlong on the floor. His head struck hard and he lost consciousness.

The next morning, as soon as Sinette had unbolted the ground floor doors, Desilus came to see her. She was in the dining room rolling her bed mat to carry it out for an airing in the sun, as was her habit.

"Tell me, Sinette, whatever possessed Mist' Dutilleul that he should act so strangely last night?" the hired man asked. "Around midnight, when the Cigouave came, I heard him fire twice. A little later I heard his screams and cries for help. He sounded like some poor wretch frightened out of his wits. Tell me, how much did he drink last night?"

The firm, opulent breasts of the maid rose and fell with a heavy sigh.

"Oh Desilus, don't speak to me of it! You know, he fell down again as he did last time. But before he collapsed I heard a strange scuffle up there. He ran wildly to every corner of the garret. It almost seemed as though he were engaged in a violent struggle with someone stronger than he."

"My God!" exclaimed the hired man. "You don't mean it, Sinette! It can't be true!"

"Oh yes, Desilus, I swear it was so. You can believe me, too. I didn't close my eyes a single second all night long! I trembled like a forest leaf. I felt something unnatural was going on up there in the garret. I even thought that the Cigouave might have come to devour Mast' Dutilleul. I lay there expecting to see the beast leaping down the stairs at any moment to gobble me up in turn. I wanted to shout for help, but I couldn't. I couldn't force a sound from my lips."

"Sinette, I swear to you . . ." the hired man babbled, abashed, "I would have come of my own accord to save you, as sure as I stand here before you. But with that 'thing' loping around the courtyard, how could I ever reach the house? Imagine yourself in my position. . . ."

"Don't worry yourself about it now, Desilus, I understand. Of course you couldn't come. It would have been impossible for you to even step outside. How could you have found the strength and courage when even Mast' Dutilleul himself was disturbed by the Cigouave? And he fears nothing, not even the Good Lord."

"Speaking of the Master, isn't he up yet?"

"Oh yes, he's already up and about. Only a little while ago I brought him his coffee. When I knocked on the door, he said he would come down and take it here. His voice sounded very queer. It sounded as though he had a hot potato on his tongue. But from what I could hear I know he was rinsing his mouth and brushing his teeth like mad trying to get rid of the evil taste of rum. Since then I've heard him pacing back and forth up there like a caged lion, as he does whenever he's angry or when he's eating his heart out thinking of Madame Dutilleul, rest her soul!"

"Well, that's good. But tell me, Sinette, do you think he might be more ferocious than usual this morning?"

"No doubt about that, Desilus! After such a horrible night as this. . . . Don't you remember what we caught for going up to take care of him the last time he collapsed on the floor?"

Desilus' face grew long.

"Sinette, you know the big foreign hog which Mist' Dutilleul bought the week before last? Well, last night the Cigouave slashed open its belly and almost completely devoured it!"

"Oh, oh! You don't say, Desilus!"

"Ah, Sinette, how I wish it weren't so! . . . I don't know how to begin to tell it to the boss. And especially now, in the state he must be in this morning!"

The maid became dejected too, thinking of the scene that would doubtless follow.

"Desilus," she said with tears in her eyes, "I think I'll have to leave this place. I would have done so long ago if my courage hadn't failed me. But now I've had more than I can stand. I don't live any more, day or night. I'm scared all the time. And when it isn't Mast' Dutilleul who would like to tear us into little pieces, it's the Cigouave. Don't you think that's enough to drive me crazy?"

"But Sinette, you can't leave Mist' Dutilleul like that. An evil fate has marked you too. You could try to go anywhere you like, but this calamity will follow you everywhere. Believe me. . . ."

He shook his head dubiously, and clicked his tongue. He thought with pity that this young woman lacked experience.

"Believe me, Sinette. I am older than you. I have seen many things. If I tell you that you can't leave, it's because I know why. By remaining here you can fix up everything. You need only close your eyes, put your problem in Rossini's hands and rely on him. He'll work for you and, thanks to his help, Mist' Dutilleul will return to your arms. Then he will only look at things through you, and in that way you will be able to change him. You will make him serve his tribal gods, and when he has settled his accounts with the loas, Bossuet will be powerless to harm anyone on this place. And then we will hear no more of the Cigouave. . . ."

He abruptly fell silent. Morin Dutilleul, his head wrapped in bandages, had appeared on the staircase. Sinette grabbed up her mat, thrust it under her arm and rushed outside. . . .

The servants had not been wrong. The Master was certainly in an ugly mood that morning. Desilus noticed it the moment he appeared. From the way Morin stared at him and from the tight line of his lips, he immediately understood that things were going to go badly for him. He knew from sad experience. But his fear would have changed to compassion had he been able to guess that this anger arose more from the shame his master felt because his servants knew that he had been drunk again than from his habitual grouchiness. For Morin was certain that they had heard and understood everything. And what really aggravated his irritation was that the bandage he wore around his head showed clearly that he had fallen as he had done once before.

Moreover, he was angry with them for having caused him, by their continual repetition of this absurd fable, to see the Cigouave in his hallucinating delirium. However, this time his scepticism had been really shaken. So strong had been his emotions of the night before that he believed, despite his better judgment, that perhaps his senses had not been deluded. He thrust this idea from his mind, but try as he would, it immediately returned. And this also added to his irritation.

If only Desilus had been able to read these inner thoughts of his master, he certainly would not have told him everything right out. But anxious to get it out of his system as quickly as possible, he told Morin that the Cigouave had killed and devoured the foreign-bred boar. It would have been better had he insinuated, in his usual prudently distorted phrases, clouded by vague allusions and foggy asides, that robbers from some district far distant from Musseau had done it. He would nevertheless have been scolded, but it would not have been as violent as the tongue lashing he caught for saying what he believed to be the truth.

At this mention of the beast Morin turned livid, seized him by the collar, shook him brutally and finally slapped his face. Poor Desilus, whipped, bruised and humiliated, broke into tears without the slightest reaction of revolt. Not that he was incapable of reacting; there were times, sometimes at the slightest offense, when he would see red. It merely proved that the patience of this black peasant was profound and that the ill-treatment of his master had not yet filled his cup to overflowing.

The pitiable attitude of his hired man, however, made Morin ashamed of his brutality. But not knowing how to withdraw from this odious situation into which his abnormal behavior had dragged him, and not daring to blame his conduct on Desilus' stupidity as he would have liked to do, Morin gruffly ordered him to fetch the justice of the peace. He had to let his fury work itself out somehow, and he understood that this time he had gone too far with his own servant. Now it was necessary to take it out on someone else. Desilus, who immediately recovered from his emotions, and also sensed the motive behind Morin's request, tried to persuade him that Sheriff Delice was helpless to do anything in a matter which concerned the Cigouave. Naturally, this only further exasperated his employer.

"That's enough out of you!" he shouted, stamping his foot. Desilus, cowed, hastened to obey, stooping under the burden of his troubles.

As he went out Sinette brought the morning coffee to Morin. He served himself without looking at her, for his hands trembled under the combined effects of the alcohol and his anger. She stood close beside him, but at a respectable distance, holding the coffee service in her hands and fearfully awaiting his orders in silence. When he finished the first cup she timidly asked if he would take another. Although he wanted more he motioned her away, for he was afraid he might spill it in her presence.

"You'd think I'd beaten my own father and mother!" poor Desilus said aloud to himself as he walked along to Delisca's house. "As if I didn't bear a heavy enough burden with this son who is sucking the marrow of my bones! And now here I am in the service of a man who has a curse on him; a man who has already drawn calamity down upon all of us here in Musseau! And he dares, at such a time, to raise his hand and strike me!"

Such a heavy run of bad luck seemed extraordinary to him, although his simple understanding furnished him with all sorts of explanations, all of them supernatural. The future seemed very black indeed to him, and it was a future which bordered on the immediate present. The future was the task of bringing the justice of the peace to see Morin Dutilleul. He was not sure he could accomplish this feat, for he doubted that Sheriff Delice would consent to visit his master's home after everything that had happened.

He found the justice in his garden, hoeing his potato patch.

"Good day, Sheriff," he called out, respectfully touching the rim of his hat.

"Why, good day, Desilus," Delisca answered cheerfully. "And how does your body feel today?"

"Ah Sheriff, my body's not well today. It's not at all well! If I were to explain it you wouldn't want to believe me; but from day to day my energy sinks lower and lower. My strength is ebbing away; it flows out of me! One would think that only wind remained in my bones, where the marrow once had been. . . . It's my very own little son who brings this on me; it is indeed! He wasn't Bossuet's godson for nothing. He inherited his taste for doing evil from the dripping candle his godfather carried at his baptism."

"How can one ever know?" Delisca agreed. "A man makes his own children, but he does not give them their senses. That is why it is always so important to select honest people to be their godfather and godmother. For it is through baptism that they acquire their qualities and their faults. . . ."

The justice of the peace had launched into one of those interminable philosophical disquisitions for which he had such an uncontrollable bent. Fearing that if he let him go on he would have to listen to him for another quarter of an hour, Desilus interrupted him, although he was sorry to be so impolite.

"Excuse me, Sheriff, if I break in on you. But Mist' Dutilleul sent me over to ask you if you could go to see him this very morning."

"Master Morin!" exclaimed the justice of the peace, astonished. "And what does he want of me?"

He squinted up at the hired man with an air of suspicion.

"You know," the latter adroitly began, "when a man holds a position of authority, he is the slave of duty. If it were otherwise nothing would run in the area he commands."

"So what has happened now?" Delisca asked impatiently, for this cautious preamble warned him there was trouble ahead.

"It's the Cigouave again, Sheriff. It came to Mist' Dutilleul's place again last night and devoured the big foreign boar he recently bought at such a high price."

"But what has a matter of that kind got to do with me?" Delisca was irritated. "I'm not a houngan. I'm only an officer of the rural police."

"That's just why Mist' Dutilleul sent me to see you. He doesn't want to hear a word about the Cigouave. He doesn't believe that this 'thing' exists. He says it must have been robbers who killed the hog and carried off the meat."

Delisca was annoyed. He shook his head and raised his arms to heaven.

"Desilus, tell me if you don't agree that this job of justice of the peace also has a curse on it?"

"Sheriff, Mist' Dutilleul and you are both big Negroes;

you're important people. Me, Desilus, poor devil that I am, I'm nothing at all. I'm not as important as a little lump of earth." He kicked a clod in the potato patch. "If you don't go to see my master, as he asks, I'm the one who will have to pay for it. He'll say like a flash that I didn't deliver his message."

The justice of the peace sighed.

"Ever since Master Morin came and settled down in Musseau everything has turned topsy-turvy. Right now they're upside down!"

've only heard rumors that you were the justice of the peace around here!" Morin greeted Delisca with these words, pronounced with bitter sarcasm. The latter spluttered with rage.

"What do you mean, Master?"

"Hold your tongue!" Morin cut him short, his voice hard and dry. "Don't you see that I'm speaking, imbecile? I tell you that I can't see that you maintain any order whatever in Musseau. Everyone treats me with disrespect. All you do is babble! Yes, and as for prattling I have to admit you can gossip better than anyone I ever met. You never do anything else. You're just like an old woman!"

"Master—"

"I'm still speaking! The night before last a man was attacked and bitten near the spring by a dog which some scoundrel set upon him. You not only have not had him taken to the hospital; you have not even made a report to the police authorities. And now we find that robbers have broken into my property. They have killed a fine foreign-bred hog that I had just bought!"

Delisca feigned surprise.

"Oh-ho, Master, what's that you say? Someone killed your little pig?"

"What," shouted Morin, "you mean to say that Desilus didn't tell you about it yet?"

He turned on the hired man furiously.

"Then I'll tell you too. You're an imbecile!"

"But, Mist' Dutilleul!—" Desilus began.

Morin brutally interrupted him.

"Enough! Shut your mouth! . . . Yes, I repeat it, you are an imbecile! I'm beginning to ask myself if you don't believe that I put money into your pocket at the end of each month for the sole pleasure of having your handsome face around, or perhaps so you can go gamble, drink and smoke it all away to remain happy!"

"Mist' Dutilleul!" poor Desilus said proudly, this time feeling his honor attacked. "Mist' Dutilleul, you can search throughout Musseau, and you will not find a better worker than I am."

"I feel no need to learn the tune you're singing now. Instead, just answer a few simple questions: When I took you to work my land for me, was it not understood that you would guard it as well?"

"Yes, Mist' Dutilleul. But—"

"There are no ifs or buts. Were you about to repeat to me again that it was the Cigouave that devoured my hog?"

"Mist'—"

" 'Mist' what? You are here to watch over my plantation. If I lose anything, you are responsible for it. And so I'm going to deduct from your pay every month until the whole sum that I paid for that fine hog has been paid back."

Desilus bowed his head, vanquished and crestfallen. How could Morin do this to him, when he hardly earned enough to live on?

"That's enough for you. And now as for you, Sheriff Delice," Morin resumed, turning to the justice of the peace, "isn't the entire region under your jurisdiction?"

"That's right."

"Very well! Then I warn you once and for all: if these disorders continue around here I am going to complain to the central police authorities. They will strip you of your rank and office. There! I have nothing more to say to you."

"Master Morin, you have spoken and I have listened to you. Now let me explain things to you for a minute or so."

"Go ahead, I'm listening."

"Master, you are an educated man, while I am only an ignorant Negro. But there is one thing I know well. I know the law."

"Ah! So you really know it!"

"Yes, I know it. For ten years now, I have been justice of the peace in Musseau. You can ask anyone hereabouts if I have not always done my duty. They will tell you what kind of a man bears the name of Delisca Delice . . . Good! I am an officer of the rural police service. A robber enters upon your property, he pillages you. What must I do? I must arrest him, tie him up, beat him with my club and then drag him to town, to the headquarters of the rural police. That is what the law commands me to do in a case like that.

"But the law does not speak of evil spirits. If the jungle gods are discontented with the people around here, and they send bad spirits to plague our district, what do you, in your innermost soul and conscience, expect a justice of the peace to do about that?"

Morin heaved a deep sigh. The arguments employed

by Sheriff Delice literally broke his back. "It would be impossible to make this dumb idiot understand anything!" he said to himself.

"Master!" resumed Delisca, imperturbably, "you have a clear mind. You tell me what I should do, and I will do it. As for myself, I know only one thing; and that is that all the tribulations which shower down upon us at this moment come from evil spirits who have sown them in our path because they are not content with us. And also because there are certain people in Musseau who are not conducting themselves properly."

"Very well, then why the devil don't you arrest them, those people?" Morin demanded.

"Master, I should like nothing better than to do just that. But I don't know who they are."

"Enough!" Morin shouted. "Get out of here! Show me your heels! I've heard enough of your stupid nonsense!"

The general store was empty. The justice of the peace knocked discreetly at the door.

"Honor!" he called.

No one answered him.

"I said 'Honor'!" he called more loudly.

"Respect!" came Madan Horace's response from her room, as she was aroused from the tenacious arms of sleep.

She finally appeared in the shop, her face pale and unkempt, her enormous protruding belly lifting her dress as high as her knees, her stockings hanging in disorder around her dirty slippers.

"Good day, Sheriff," she murmured, in a voice filled with lassitude.

Then, astonished at not seeing her goddaughters in the shop, which she had placed in their charge, she aroused herself.

"Those little sluts have run off in heat again! They haven't even matured and they're already chasing after the men! Sheriff, tell me what is wrong with them! In my condition I no longer have the strength to correct them. When Horace returns this evening I'll speak to him and have him skin them alive with a tough switch!"

Delisca uttered a deep sigh.

"There is a proverb which says: impudent children grow up under the sod. But indeed, that's the way they all are these days. There are moments, Madan Horace, when I ask myself if someone hasn't turned the world inside out. Just look at the things that are happening in Musseau right now, and then tell me if it isn't so!"

"Please don't talk that way, Sheriff! . . . Do you know the agony we lived through last night?"

She related to him that the Cigouave had run amuck like a fury in their courtyard until dawn, howling, barking and scratching at the doors of the house. And all the while he was there they heard the infernal noise of chains and pots and pans being dragged about on the ground. Horace had gotten up, recited prayers, and sprinkled the house with holy water, but without success.

"And the whistle?" asked the justice of the peace.

"What whistle, Sheriff?" she asked him in amazement.

"But every time the 'thing' comes people say they always hear whistle blasts at the same time. That's what everyone has told me. Ti-Charles heard them, Desilus and Master Morin also heard them."

"Well now, Sheriff, I don't know a thing you're talking about. Neither Horace nor myself have heard any whistles. And yet the 'thing' persecuted us all night long."

She lied, knowing very well that Bossuet was suspected of guiding the beast. She didn't, of course, doubt in the least that he was. But she would not have admitted the wrongs of her relatives for anything in the world, no matter how flagrant they might be. Had she done so, she would have felt that she had failed in the sacred duties of family solidarity.

"All night long!" she resumed. "See how bloodshot my eyes are! I was able to close them only with the dawn, this morning. But that isn't all, Sheriff. Do you realize that Horace even blamed me for this visit? Imagine! He said that if I had not gone to Ti-Charles' cabin with the houngan, the 'thing' would not have returned to our house to cause us this trouble. But tell me, could I have abandoned my little brother to his misfortune, when Madan Bossuet has not even put her foot inside his door to see what condition he was in, nor simply come to ask about him!"

Delisca Delice did not answer her. He was bitterly mulling over the scene Morin Dutilleul had made for him. In view of the respectable position he held in the community it could only be described as odious.

"Sheriff," asked Madan Horace, disturbed by his silence, "is there anything wrong with you? I find you very upset this morning."

He glanced at the shopkeeper and hesitated an instant before answering her.

"You know, Madan Horace," he finally said, speaking slowly and soberly, "I believe that I shall be obliged to hand in my resignation."

Madan Horace jumped.

"What can you be saying, Sheriff? It can't be that I have heard you aright. You mean you intend to quit your post? But then, what would happen to us here in Musseau when you are no longer in command of the district?"

"You might as well know all about it, Madan Horace . . . Throughout the long period I have been an officer of the rural police, nobody here has ever made the slightest reproach to me. Not a single complaint as big as that!" And he showed the nail on his little finger.

"Oh, no, Sheriff! No, no, no! As for that . . ."

"Very well! But from the day that Master Morin came to settle down in the district a whole series of tribulations have fallen upon me."

"Not only on you, Sheriff. I think everybody around here has also been troubled."

"Madan Horace, I am a man of a certain age. Just look at my hairs; by now they have all turned white. I have seen many things in my day, lots and lots of them! But in all my days I have never seen the likes of what I am going through now in Musseau! Wherever he came from, Master Morin came here with a curse upon his head. He sought a quarrel with Bossuet, who was half looking for it anyway. Bossuet didn't hesitate one instant. He immediately roused up the Cigouave and unleashed it in the very heart of the community."

Madan Horace raised her hands to her eyes.

"Bossuet! Oh, don't say such a thing, Sheriff. Don't!"

But Delisca pretended not to hear her. He continued:

"And as for Master Morin, he puts on his airs of a foreign white man who doesn't know anything about the real conditions in Haiti! He sends Desilus to fetch me, to tell me, as if he were accusing me, that he has lost a boar. I answer by telling him that it's the Cigouave who devoured his little pig. He will hear nothing of it! He declares that I am responsible and that if some people do bad things that arouse the anger of the loas, I must arrest them. One would think that he was not the one who chopped down the mapou tree of All-Merciful Legba!"

"Is this what he said to you, Sheriff? But you should know by now that Master Morin hasn't got a penny's worth of honesty in him, no sir! And he'll stand by and watch innocent people killed for nothing, one of these days!"

"There's no doubt of it, Madan Horace! He's capable of doing just that. But that wasn't all he said to me. Do you know what he threatened to do to me, just a little while ago? He said that if I did not put an end to the disorders in Musseau, he would go straight to the authorities at rural police headquarters and demand that I be dismissed!"

"My God! . . . What misery is this that he wishes upon you, Sheriff? Don't you believe that this mulatto has gone stark, raving mad?"

The justice of the peace only shrugged his shoulders, shook his head and spat far out on the dusty road. It was enough to show the disdain with which he regarded Morin Dutilleul.

"Madan Horace," he said solemnly, getting up, "as sure as I stand here before you, I have never wished evil on any man. But I can only remind you of the proverb which says: 'The bull shits, thinking he will soil the pasture, but he only dirties his own hind quarters.' "

And with that he stalked out of the store.

O ne afternoon Irma went to the cabin of her fiancé, although she had been expressly forbidden to do so by her father. Madan Horace, who was washing her brother's linen in the courtyard, not far from the veranda, waved to the girl that she could go in.

Ti-Charles dozed, his body quivering from time to time with a low, feeble sob. For some days now, despite Rossini's care, his condition had worsened. His wounds were now running sores, giving off an atrocious odor of decay which attracted the flies. The poor boy had lost all hope and awaited death. A high fever kept him in a condition verging on stupor.

The young woman crossed the threshold with hesitating footsteps, then wavered, holding her nose as the stench hit her. At the same instant, as though he divined her presence, poor Ti-Charles' eyes fluttered open. Ashamed at the sight of his beloved trembling there before him in his lamentable state, he quickly turned his face to the wall. Irma wrung her hands. She felt a lump in her throat.

"Ti-Charles!" she called, in a stifled voice.

As he did not answer she grew more determined. She advanced stiffly, knelt down beside his sickbed, and kissed his forehead. He took her hand tenderly, without saying a word, and without looking up. She sighed.

"Father forbade me to come. That's why I didn't come sooner," she said in a low voice. "But I felt such a desire to see you that I came. It was stronger than myself."

"I know. But Alcaeus was right. You should have listened to him, Irma. I didn't want you to see me in this sad condition. But since you are here, dearest, I must tell you the truth. . . . Bossuet has won his game . . . As things now stand . . . I . . ."

He raised his head slightly, fixing his eyes upon the girl in a strange, haggard look.

"You must no longer think of me, Irma . . . because . . . now everything is finished . . . everything!"

Hearing these words of despair, she stood up brusquely, raised her hand to her heart and collapsed in a heap on the hard dirt floor. Madan Horace came running at her brother's call for help. He had tried, in a foolish reflex action, to rise and go to the rescue of his fiancée. Now he twisted and turned on his bed from rage and pain, and cried bitterly.

"Oh-ho!" the shopkeeper exclaimed, seeing the girl lying on the floor. "What can have happened here?"

Without waiting for Ti-Charles' answer, she seized the cut-glass bottle from the table and dashed its contents into Irma's face. Then she slapped her vigorously. Irma recovered quickly. As soon as she opened her eyes, her first words were for her lover.

"Ti-Charles!" she cried plaintively, her gaze wandering. "Ti-Charles! Where is he?"

"Where else do you think he could be," the shopkeeper answered, shrugging her shoulders, "except in his bed?"

She helped Irma to her feet, and as the girl immediately burst into tears, she held her around the waist and spoke softly to her.

"My child, you shouldn't stay here. Come! Come with me."

"No, Madan Horace," Irma protested. "No, I don't want to leave . . . My place now is here beside Ti-Charles. And if he should die, I will kill myself and follow him into the earth."

Ti-Charles forced himself to smile at her.

"And whoever told you that I was going to die, Irma?"

"What!" the young girl exclaimed. "But you yourself told me. Only a few minutes ago you said to me that everything was finished."

"Yes, that's true, my beloved," the young man replied, "but that was just a remark. I didn't mean it. I didn't expect to see you at all, and when you suddenly appeared I was so surprised that I talked nonsense. Those were only the words of a man in fever . . . Rossini said only yesterday that in a few more hours I would be able to get up . . . And then I will come to see you every evening at dusk, as we used to do before. . . ."

Irma could hardly believe her ears, but, clutching at this fragile hope that Charles held out to her in pity for her weakness, she pleaded: "Is it true, Ti-Charles? Do you mean it? You're not lying to me?"

"May the Virgin hear me, I am not lying to you!" he answered, nodding his head in vigorous affirmation.

She moved close to him again, took his head in her arms and covered it with kisses. When she stopped to recover her breath, Ti-Charles said to her, smiling:

"Now you should go, for it is better, for both you and me, that you do not remain here. Just see how you fainted a moment ago. If my sister hadn't been there to come to your aid, you might have died before my very eyes."

Madan Horace took the girl's arm affectionately.

"Now that's enough talk, my friends!" she said firmly.
"Come with me, Irma, come along now! I'll accompany
you part of the way home."

Irma let herself be led off without resisting. But as she
crossed the threshold she stifled a sob, so that her lover
would not hear her crying.

Ti-Charles was no less depressed than she. Hardly had
the two women left the courtyard than the young man,
giving way to despair, struggled upright on his couch, and
groped for the cut-glass bottle which lay on the floor
within reach. Summoning all his energy, he smashed it on
the hard earth. Then, without hesitation, he took a sharp
piece of the broken glass and slashed his throat. . . .

Meeting the justice of the peace on the road as he was making his rounds of the village, Madan Horace begged him
to accompany Irma to her parents. Delisca hesitated
briefly, tempted to refuse because he was on duty, but
finally put his arm in a fatherly manner on her shoulders
and escorted her home.

Moved by her obvious distress, which he understood
—for he had learned how to sympathize with others in
order to be just in the performance of his duties—he did
his best to console her. But Irma was so upset that she did
not hear his kind words and was hardly calmed by them.

Ti-Charles is going to die, she thought to herself. I
know he is. He lied to me. It isn't true that he will soon
be better, and he knew it all the time. . . .

Meanwhile Madan Horace had returned to her brother's
hovel. At the sight of the suicide lying in a vast pool of
blood in the last throes of death—for his agony had been

long—she aroused the neighbors with a torrent of shrieks and screams.

People came running from all directions. They found her rolling on the ground, without the slightest care for her own pregnant condition, her eyes staring from their sockets, tearing out her hair and slashing at the hard earth with her nails. For now she was only a woman in sorrow, and like all women through the ages, despite the blackness of her skin, she reacted as Hecuba had done, in the age of Homer.

Men tried in vain to pin her down and hold her still. The women, following the ancient custom of mourners, encouraged her despair with funereal laments, so that the deceased, receiving his due share of mourning, should not later have anything for which to reproach them.

The scene reached a paroxysm of fury when Bossuet's wife, Sor Cie, attracted by the uproar, arrived in her turn. Madan Horace, blinded by disaster, threw all family decorum to the winds. She tore herself loose from the hands of those trying to calm her, leaped at the throat of his sister-in-law, tore the bandana from her head, scratched her face, and all the while screamed curses on her at the top of her lungs. And she cursed Bossuet, her own brother, as well.

"Tribe of madmen!" she screamed. "You already killed Ferdinand! But that wasn't enough for you. Today it's Ti-Charles you have chosen to kill. And tomorrow it will be the infant I bear in my womb. . . ."

Men tried to come between the two women, but the shopkeeper had found the strength of lions and clung to her victim. By now poor Sor Cie was stripped almost naked and her entire body was covered with long scarlet scratches from which the blood flowed. One of her eyes was swollen and disfigured. . . .

"Give me a knife so I can rip out her guts!" howled Madan Horace.

But after repeated efforts the men finally succeeded in overpowering her. And Bossuet's wife, without waiting for an explanation, took to her heels and fled, the torn shreds of her clothing flapping grotesquely behind her. She did not even bother to bind up her breasts, which bounced about loosely under her torn blouse.

When Horace and the justice of the peace, who had been urgently summoned, reached the scene, the shopkeeper, worn out by her raving outbursts, considered them an instant with a sullen and ferocious stare. Then, pointing to the corpse of her young brother, she moaned.

"Gaze upon the work of Bossuet, my friends! Just look!"

Horace murmured a short prayer over the limp body of Ti-Charles, whom he had loved like his own son, then closed the staring eyes and placed a crucifix on Charles' breast. He poured holy water into a dish, placed a sprig of fresh boxwood in it, and set them upon a chair beside the pallet of the dead man.

"The Lord is merciful," he concluded with pious resignation, and with the satisfaction of a duty accomplished. "He will pardon your sins, little brother. May you rest in peace! Amen!"

Ti-Charles' wake was one of the saddest ever celebrated in Musseau. Few people attended it. Hymns were sung, and prayers recited; but contrary to native custom, there was no funeral feast and no entertainment. Two kerosene lamps burned fitfully and smokily, feebly lighting up the interior of the cabin with a tawny, murky light. Several bottles of white rum were placed on the table, together with some white enamel coffeepots and some cups and glasses, but nobody drank. Everybody was depressed. Everyone, even the justice of the peace, seemed to be waiting for some strange and terrifying thing to happen. None of the guests would probably have stayed for the wake if it had not been for a feeling of duty and pity which Madan Horace's condition aroused in them.

The poor woman squatted on the hard earth floor of the hut. Cupping her head in her hands, she obstinately stared at the body of her brother, whose face was fixed in a smile of happy repose. In it was frozen for all time the ardent simplicity and beauty which once had turned the heads of all the young women in the district. Even the bandage which bound up his jaws, and the cotton wads which had been plugged into his nostrils and ears, did not detract from his manly beauty. Madan Horace neither sang nor prayed; either of which would have appeared more natural. But from time to time a hearbreaking cry burst from her, causing everyone to shudder. Then she lapsed again into her mournful contemplation of the dead boy.

Shortly before midnight a dwarf clothed and capped all in white passed by on the highway. He looked like a night watchman making his rounds.

"Mast' Calfou!" the justice of the peace, who was standing on the veranda, muttered hoarsely.

"Yes, Sheriff," his adjutant Polycarp agreed, "that's him all right. It's been a long time since we've seen him in this section. And the Good Lord knows how much we need his presence to protect us from this 'thing' which Bossuet has unleashed on Musseau. Since he seems to be inspecting the district, I should like to believe that this night at least we shall not see the Cigouave. Unless the man should prove more powerful than he. Bossuet has such great powers that I even wouldn't be surprised to see such a good spirit as Mast' Calfou reach an agreement with him!"

"Don't talk such nonsense!" said the justice of the peace testily. "Mast' Calfou never makes friends with those who work only with their left hand. And that is why he is out on the highways and byways every evening, for his role is to prevent anyone from doing evil at any of the cross-roads. . . ."

"But, Sheriff!" protested an old man, "you know very well that you need only 'pay' Mast' Calfou for him to shut his eyes to anything that might happen. And more-over, as a matter of fact, no spirit is completely good nor bad. It is only living Christians who persuade them to do evil things. People nowadays have such a lust for money! It was not like this . . ."

He didn't have time to conclude his little speech. As though to prove him right, the sinister blast of a whistle tore to shreds the hot and black silence of this tragic night. And instantly all things grew still. The snakes, the birds, the insects stirred no more. And even the plants stopped growing and stiffened their branches, lest their leaves might rustle in the night. Soon after, the howls of the strange beast pierced the still night air, as it had done on all the previous nights.

Instantly there was an indescribable tumult among the mourners gathered on the veranda and inside the cabin.

Those inside frantically closed and bolted the door. Those outside, seeing their escape barred, crowded against the door and hammered on it, swearing and pleading to get in. The justice of the peace was not the least excited among them.

"Open, my friends, please open the door!" he pleaded. "It is me, Delisca Delice, your chief, who commands you to let us in."

But inside nobody heard him, because of the shrill lamentations which arose from the women, and the thunderous pounding on the door.

Suddenly Horace asked: "But where is Sheriff Delice?"

Realizing that he had been left outside, the carpenter bravely made his way through the throng to open the door for the justice of the peace. The others protested, and as Horace seemed determined to go on, they tried to bar his way. But he was firm and brushed aside the trembling hands that tried to hold him back.

He had barely pushed back the bolt than those outside violently tore open the door and tumbled into the room, with Delisca right in front of them. It had happened just in time, for the howls of the beast came nearer and nearer and it was clear that he would soon enter the courtyard of dead Ti-Charles' home.

Although the body had been carefully prepared for burial (someone had even gone to the trouble of inserting congo pea leaves in his open, festering wounds), it was decomposing rapidly in the oppressive heat. In the stifling closeness of the crowded room, heated even more by the tightly pressed bodies, all trembling and sweating with the agony of terror, a sickening odor of decay and putrefaction pervaded the air. Horace thought it would be good to open a window for a second to freshen the room. But one look at the haggard, terror-stricken faces of his guests was enough to make him understand that this time they would never let him reach a window.

Moreover, by this time the beast had entered the court-yard itself. . . .

adan Horace insisted on attending the funeral of her younger brother, despite the advice of her husband and friends. Returning on foot from the Delmas cemetery in the sweltering heat, she was stricken by a serious hemorrhage. For a time her life trembled in the balance and it seemed that the evil forebodings which had plagued her so long might be confirmed.

Since then she had been confined to her bed, lying propped up so that her feet were higher than her head.

As a further precaution Sor Ti-Ma, the midwife of Musseau, had bound a dried umbilical cord around her waist and placed a poultice mixed with starch, the white of an egg, and elm bark on her swollen belly.

Horace, although he appreciated this treatment, was not satisfied and frequently pleaded with the Good Lord to save his wife. He reported to him, in vehement language, all the evil acts of Bossuet and begged him to cast that scoundrel once and for all into the eternal flames of hell. And he sprinkled the corners of the house and of the yard with holy water each morning and evening in order to drive off all evil spirits.

Everything seemed to have taken a turn for the better when one night Madan Horace again saw in her dreams the old Negress who had previously come to warn her that someone in her family was trying to harm her.

"Elise," the mysterious woman called to her. "Elise, I already warned you what you must do to save your infant. You did not follow my instructions. You listened to Horace, who is an old imbecile. It's just too bad for you, my daughter. Now you can anchor down your belly and scream for help, for all the good that will do. You are about to lose your little one. And when that happens you will know that it was your own fault, for I warned you."

The shopkeeper awoke with a start, bathed in a sweat of fear and uttering animallike cries. Her husband, to whom she related her dream, vainly tried to reason with her.

"But, Elise, can't you see that it is simply the devil who is trying to torment you?" he told her. "Be calm, Sor Elise. The Lord is with us. And as we have never done Him any wrong, He will not abandon us in our trial. He will answer our prayers, as He has always done before."

But she was not at all reassured. She passed the remainder of that night in a state of extreme agitation and at the break of dawn she was seized by violent cramps.

Informed by Madan Horace's god daughters, their neighbors flocked to the house and soon it was filled to overflowing. Soon the men joined the cackling flock of women, and even the justice of the peace graced the household with his presence.

Although he believed in the infinite bounty of Almighty God, who reigns over all things on earth as well as in heaven, Horace lost all his self-control with the first birth pangs of his wife. Finding him in this sorry condition, Sheriff Delice took control of everything, for he never lacked power of decision. He ordered the men to leave the house and to stay on the veranda. And then he pushed the most talkative and useless wives out with them. He ordered those who remained to heat some water on the fire, and sent Polycarp, his adjutant, to fetch Sor Ti-Ma, the village midwife.

She soon arrived, puffing and blowing in her haste. She was a big Negress with an authoritative face, whose imposing corpulence commanded respect. She was covered with heavy rolls of fat, which bulged under her showy clothes, clearly proving that she lived in honorable abundance and had never suffered hunger.

Conscious of her own importance, she hardly deigned to acknowledge the greetings of those present. She walked majestically straight to the bed of the woman in childbirth. She carried with her the articles of her profession in a palm-straw sack which contained various medicinal herbs, amulets and a kitchen knife, well sharpened, to cut the umbilical cord.

She lost no time in completing all preparations for the delivery. She stripped the shopkeeper of all clothing and, in order to prevent her from catching cold during her delivery, bound a towel around her chest. She gave her a hot cinnamon toddy, and then, placing a low chair under the pillows, she made the patient squat, half-upright, upon it, with her legs spread wide, in the position known as "sitting on little stumps." After this was accomplished she soaked her midwife's hands in palm oil and vigorously massaged Madan Horace's belly and anointed her private parts, while the latter shrieked like a wounded animal.

In the midst of her exertions the poor woman's face was beaded with great drops of sweat. She drew her breath in deep wheezing gasps and puffed like a foundry bellows. Her eyes dilated with suffering and terror. As though torn by her efforts, at each contraction of her abdominal muscles she gave off a flow of discharge streaked with blood.

"Push!" Sor Ti-Ma patiently urged her on. "Keep pushing, Madan Horace! Push hard!"

And the shopkeeper, suffocating, her mouth distorted with pain, tried her best to comply, in the hope of an early delivery. Horace stood gaping. Broken in anguish over his powerlessness to help her, clammy and shivering like a man in fever, he watched the scene with a stupid air. Nobody had seen Horace like this before. They knew him only as a man whose faith seemed firmly anchored and who always had the name of the Good Lord on his lips. Struck by his confusion, the justice of the peace put his arm around his shoulder and led him to the door.

"Come with me, friend Horace," he said softly to him. "Come! It is not good for a man to remain, as you are doing, in the same room where his wife is in the midst of her birth pains. It is said always to bring bad luck."

The carpenter let himself be led away submissively. When they were outside the room and in the shop, Sheriff Delice poured him two fingers of rum. Horace drank it mechanically, without wryly grimacing as usual, and then collapsed into a chair. His face was twisted into a painful expression of stupidity. To bolster up his spirits, Delisca explained to him that all women in childbirth went through the same suffering he had seen in his wife. But Horace did not hear a word he said. His lower lip trembled convulsively, and he was shaken by a confused and completely animal terror, of which he was hardly conscious.

"My Lord God!" he would sigh now and then. But his mind moved no further.

Sheriff Delice finally grew annoyed at such a show of weakness.

"Friend Horace, are you a man or aren't you?" he asked brusquely. "Come now, let us see you give some sign of life! You've collapsed like a scarecrow with straw guts! Arouse yourself a little!"

Nevertheless, despite the roughness of his rebukes, the justice of the peace was worried too. But his fears were not caused by the screams nor the suffering of the woman in childbirth, for he knew these things to be normal. He simply had a premonition that some further calamity was about to occur. The shopkeeper had not taken the bath prescribed in her dream, and, moreover, Master Morin had drawn down the angry curse of Almighty Legba upon all the inhabitants of Musseau. Not to mention the black activities of Bossuet, who had unleashed the Cigouave on the community. That very night he had heard it again howling near the spring.

He had just reached this point in his thoughts when the cries of Madan Horace suddenly ceased. The silence immediately became ominous. The justice of the peace and the carpenter instinctively listened to every sound in the other room. They could hear nothing but feeble moans and excited whispers.

What was going on in there? Why this sudden silence?

Had the child finally been delivered? Or did it mark the catastrophe so dreaded by them all, the death of Madan Horace? But then, perhaps after all she had merely fainted.

The carpenter rose to his feet and moved towards the door, like a sleepwalker in a trance. Delisca grabbed him firmly by his shirtsleeve and held him back.

"Just wait a minute, good friend Horace! Wait till they call you. They'll soon be finished."

The man mechanically sat down again. He was so limp, so thoroughly broken by the apprehensions that swept over him that he seemed utterly without will power. He buried his face in his hands and wept silently, his head empty of every thought. Not the slightest tremor ran through this strong workman's body, whose shoulders seemed so large and powerful, but which at this moment had been beaten into helplessness by his distress.

Sor Ti-Ma finally came to fetch the two men. Drawing the justice of the peace to one side she whispered to him.

"Would you believe it, Sheriff? The poor woman has not delivered her baby!"

"Mama!" Delisca exclaimed. "Oh-ho! Oh-ho! Do you mean to tell me that she simply had a windy birth."

"Windy birth, Sheriff! Do you really believe that such a thing can happen? Only city folk could invent such a silly hoax."

"Well then, Sor Ti-Ma, just tell me: If Madan Horace had carried an infant inside her, where could it have vanished?"

"How should I know, Sheriff? I only know one thing for certain, and that is that the poor woman delivered nothing more than air and blood."

"There you are! Just as I expected!" exclaimed the justice of the peace, his voice rising. "Horace is so stubborn that he never follows the good advice of others."

Excited by what he had just heard, he explained to the midwife the dream the shopkeeper had had some time before and told her how the carpenter had forbidden his wife to take the bath that the ghost of some ancestor had recommended. Sor Ti-Ma nodded her head, dismayed.

"And why, Sheriff, didn't someone call me immediately when that happened?" she demanded aloud, with great annoyance. "I could have done what was necessary to save the child. Now it is too late. The werewolves have completely devoured the infant in its mother's womb."

Horace, who heard these words pronounced at the top of her angry voice, jumped up raging, and tried to force his way into the bedroom. But Sor Ti-Ma blocked the doorway with her ample body. The justice of the peace threw his arms around the carpenter from behind and held on to him, while he struggled violently to break loose from both of them.

"Who dares to touch me in my own home?" he screamed. "How dare you show such disrespect? Truly, everyone seems to think they can order me about today. You would think I were a child, instead of the master of this house! Let me go!"

The shopkeeper, hearing her husband's outcry, also began to shout with all her strength.

"Oh, Horace! They have stolen my baby from me! They have devoured it alive in my womb!"

The women tried to calm her.

"But nobody has told you that, Madan Horace, nobody. The child is still there inside you. Soon, if you remain calm, you will deliver him."

But she wouldn't listen to them. So Sor Ti-Ma rushed back into the room, pulled a little flask containing a brown liquid from her mysterious bag, and forced the shopkeeper to swallow a tablespoon of the stuff. It was a powerful sleeping potion, which had the immediate effect of calming her. In a short while she sighed deeply and fell into slumber, despite the incessant cries of her husband who was still struggling to break free from the arms of Sheriff Delice and his adjutant, who had run in to help hold him down.

"Let go of me!" he bellowed at the top of his lungs. "You are going too far, I tell you! May the devil take you! Let go, I say!"

"Now just calm yourself, friend Horace," the justice of the peace repeated soothingly.

But alas, this kind of reasoning only enraged Horace even more.

"Shut up! The devil take you! How dare you stand there and tell me to be quiet?" he shouted rudely. "Aren't you the very people who are responsible for everything that's happened? You've served the devil so faithfully! What more could one expect?"

At last they were able to drag him out into the courtyard, where Delisca finally succeeded, not without difficulty, in pacifying him.

"Good friend Horace," he said, when they had calmed him down a little. "You shouldn't go on screaming like that! Sor Elise is sleeping now. Do you want to deprive her of rest, after all she has been through?"

The carpenter looked up at him with haggard eyes, as if he could not understand. Then, overwhelmed by a sudden attack of sobbing, he fell down on his knees and beat his breast with heavy blows of despair.

"My God," he groaned. "My God, how you have made me suffer! You have crushed me down, and yet I have never strayed from your path, I have never done evil to any man. But since you have, in your all-powerful wisdom, decided that it should be so, I can only bow to your will. I bow down low before Thee . . ."

He beat his forehead against the earth.

"Low, my Lord! . . . Very low. . . ."

The justice of the peace took him affectionately by the arm and drew him back to his feet.

"Now there, friend Horace!" he began. But he could say nothing more. For once he could not find words to express what he felt.

The carpenter raised his arms to heaven.

"May God's will be done!" he sighed, full of resignation.

Then he made the sign of the cross and entered his house.

n Morin Dutilleul's farm things were also going from bad to worse. Despite the *ouanga* charm that Rossini had prepared for Desilus—a little sachet of unbleached cloth containing various beneficent ingredients which he wore around his neck like a scapular—he had grown so stiff with rheumatism that for some time now he could only drag himself about with the aid of a cane. Morin's crops, overrun by the wild weeds which grew in profusion during the rainy season, were rapidly being choked. Aided by Sinette, the old hired man managed somehow to take care of the domestic animals, for there were fortunately few of them.

The Master no longer reproached either of them for anything. He who had always been so prompt to reprimand them, and never let the slightest occasion pass without working himself into a rage, had grown indifferent. Discouraged, or so it seemed, he took no further interest in the farm. He went into town almost every day. People said he visited the doctor, and that he was under medical treatment to break his drinking habits. Whether or not this was true, it was a fact that during this period no one saw him drunk.

Sinette, however, attributed this miraculous change to a magical powder which she had been secretly putting in his food without his ever suspecting it. A girl friend had given her the recipe. Encouraged by this first success and urged on by Desilus, whose one wish was to see her become the mistress of Dutilleul and thus rid them all of their curse, she finally forgot her religious scruples and went to visit the houngan. All she wanted was some charm which would not, however, bind her in any compact with the devil.

The matter was not so simple, Rossini told her, for he could do nothing for her without the aid of Baron Saturday. Sinette, frightened, was tempted to withdraw. But Rossini reassured her, insisting that this was an easy way of obtaining the charm, without any further obligation than the price, which was only seventeen gourds, or seventeen centimes.

"Do you have that much money on you?" he asked.

"Yes, of course," she replied. "Here it is. Desilus told me about how much I would have to give you."

Having pocketed the money, the houngan placed a sacred stone—a meteorite which once had fallen from the sky, on the earthen floor of his thatched hut—and poured some alcohol on it which he lit. Then, after reciting a short prayer in the language of the voodoo spirits, he struck three ringing blows on the meteorite with a machete. Immediately the spirit, summoned by the rites which the houngan had performed, descended into him and through his mouth said to Sinette:

"It's me, Baron Saturday himself! Baron Samedi, Baron Cemetery, Baron of the Cross, Three Shovels, Three Hoes, Three Picks! Listen well to what I am about to say. Tomorrow you must rise very early in the morning. Before speaking to anyone, you must pick seven leaves from seven different trees. Then you must prepare a bath, into which you have squeezed the juice of the leaves, and rub your whole body with this. Have you understood clearly?"

"Yes, Baron."

"You will not forget?"

"No, I will not forget."

"That's good. Now I am going to give you something else."

He took from the altar a candle of whale blubber, and cut two small notches in it with a knife. Having marked it into three equal parts, he gave it to Sinette, who took it with trembling hands.

"Now tomorrow at six o'clock in the morning, you must light this candle," he told her. "You should let it burn down to the first mark, and then you must extinguish it. You should light it again at noon, but you must put it out by the second mark. At six o'clock in the evening you should burn the rest. Have you understood clearly?"

"Yes, Baron!"

"Then, my child, try hard not to forget what I have just told you. Because if you are not careful and let the entire candle burn at one time, or if you let the flame melt it below the next mark at noon or dawn, a terrible calamity will fall upon you. You will be changed into a werewolf! And every night, at midnight, you will fly in the night air like a hoot owl! You have understood me clearly?"

"Yes, Baron," whispered Sinette, overwhelmed.

"Good. Now I shall leave you. . . ."

All went well until noon. Sinette had just relit the candle when Morin, returning from town with the appetite of a wolf, ordered her to serve his lunch. While she waited on him, she went to the kitchen from time to time to see if the candle flame had not yet reached the second notch.

Morin was irritated by the repeated comings and goings of the maid and by her extreme nervousness. So he ordered her to remain beside the table and wait on him until he had finished. She stood stock still in her confusion, finding no pretext for going out. With death in her heart, she prayed for heavenly intercession. The kitchen door stood wide open and a simple gust of wind over the spot she named would be sufficient to blow out the accursed candle of the devil at the second mark.

"Lord God!" she prayed. "Good Lord! There's a breeze blowing at this very moment, and it is such a small thing I beg of you! . . ." Only her twitching face betrayed her emotion. "Ai-ai! Virgin, full of grace! Mama! Come to my aid! Save me!"

When the moody Morin had finished and finally released her from table service she rushed into the kitchen. Alas! The candle had burned itself out. Only a tiny blackened piece of wick remained. The poor girl uttered a stifled cry, buried her head in her hands, and ran out to find the hired man.

"Whatever is wrong with you, Sinette?" Desilus asked, astonished to see her in such a state of hysteria. "Did Mist' Dutilleul slap you this time?"

"Adie, papa!" she moaned, sobbing. "If it were only that! Words are too much for me, I cannot speak . . . Ai-ai, Desilus! . . . It's the candle. The candle!"

"You let it burn out?"

"Peace, I beg of you. Peace!" she whispered, bowing her head.

"You mean to say you did that!" he groaned, raising his hand to his mouth instinctively in horror.

Then in deep anger, he went on.

"But Sinette. You mean to say . . . Couldn't you yourself . . . Look! You lit the candle, didn't you? Then you should have remained to watch it. Now if I had been in your place, thunder and lightning could strike the house, but I wouldn't have budged."

"But Desilus," the maid protested, "it wasn't my fault. Believe me! It was Mast' Dutilleul who came back from town and called me to say he was very hungry. How was it possible for me not to serve him?"

"Oh-ho, Sinette! How could you yourself say that? You mean to tell me that you couldn't even go out to the kitchen from time to time to look at the candle?"

"That's just what I tried to do. But then Mast' Dutilleul became angry and ordered me to stay there beside him. You know what he's like. . . . Now what will happen to me?"

"Very well, my girl, now you're in a fix! What can I advise you to do? Go at once to see Rossini, and ask him."

"But Desilus, what can he do for me now? Baron Saturday warned me . . . He told me that. . . ."

She couldn't find the words. Hiding her face in her hands, she stumbled off.

"Poor devil! Sinette!" sighed Desilus, "your troubles are just beginning!"

All afternoon, while Morin lay in his hammock taking a siesta, Sinette prayed to the Blessed Virgin, burning candle after candle before the image of the Holy Mother.

"I didn't want to go there! I didn't intend to do it!" she pleaded in her own simple words. "It was Desilus. Yes, it was he who got me in this fix. I told him no, it wasn't wise. But he kept on insisting, day in and day out. He did it! He did it! . . . And then, Most Merciful Virgin, dearest one!

Thou knowest, when something like that gets hammered into your head . . . So! What would you have done if you were in my place? . . . Wouldn't you have given way too? . . ."

At other moments, recalling the warning of Baron Saturday, she begged the Madonna to drag her from the claws of Satan: "Save me, Most Merciful . . . I am only a poor, unfortunate girl . . ."

Then she began praying again.

When dusk fell, the problems of her work tore her away with deep regret from this familiar conversation with the mother of Christ; but so great was her emotion that she dropped two dishes and a water jug. As the last one fell to the floor and broke into splinters, Morin grew angry.

"What's wrong with you, butterfingers?" he began.

But at that very moment the maid uttered a hoarse cry and collapsed. She felt as though a great wind raged around her, while some strange fluid, entering through the soles of her feet, forced its way into her veins. She spun around and fell with a crash to the floor. Her body jerked and trembled violently, as though seized by an epileptic convulsion. It was clearly the start of a fit of possession.

All this time she felt the strange fluid penetrating deeper and deeper into her, until it had completely invaded her whole body. And soon she felt that some strange personality was inside her, fighting with her own spirit in a struggle to subjugate her. She heard it speaking through her own mouth in a language she did not know, and saw herself acting in a way her will had not commanded.

Sinette's eyes, as round as roulette balls, seemed about to start out of her head. Her face was horribly convulsed, and she jerked, gesticulated, groaned and spoke strangely through her nose. Morin looked down upon her with some interest, mingled with surprise and fear, for this was the first time such a spectacle had taken place before his eyes. For a brief moment, if his authority had not been in question, he might even have been grateful to the maid. But when Sinetre stood up and began to walk fixedly towards him, he grew frightened and stepped back as she advanced. Finally, unable to stand it any longer, he turned and fled, running to fetch the hired man.

At the sight of Desilus who came running, Baron Saturday—for it was he who had taken possession of Sinette—appeared satisfied, finally finding himself in the presence of someone he knew. Morin was visibly an outsider, marked by his bourgeois appearance, who knew nothing of the respect and attention to which he was accustomed.

"Bring me some rum!" he ordered the hired man. And, as Desilus was about to obey, he added as an afterthought, "And also a cigar!"

Desilus lost no time fetching them. The spirit, after drinking the entire contents of the bottle, lit a cigar, drew several long puffs on it, and spat on the floor with contentment.

"I warned Sinette," he finally said, "but she would not follow my instructions. Very well! So tonight, at midnight, she will be changed into a werewolf!"

"But Baron Papa!" pleaded the hired man. "It wasn't her fault, really it wasn't."

"And why not? Didn't I already warn her?"

"Yes, you had already spoken to her, and you warned her all right! But at noon today, hardly had she lit the candle again that Mist' Dutilleul—that's him you see standing over there—he ordered her to give him something to eat. That's how it happened, I swear! So the rest of the candle burned out."

"I'm not interested in all these silly details you're telling me. Mist' Dutilleul called Sinette, that's true. I know that. But she had no reason to obey him! It was me alone that she should have served today, and not him, or any other man! So, since she did not observe my commands, this very night she shall fly. You must tell her this on my behalf."

Desilus got down on his knees, and joined his hands in supplication.

"Mercy, Baron Papa. I beg you for her sake, mercy!"

"I have never had pity on anyone in all my life," replied the Master of the Cemeteries sternly. "As I have promised, so shall it be! This very night she will change into a werewolf."

"You are so merciless, Baron. Yes, indeed!" groaned the hired man. "I swear in all my life I have never seen such a cruel, hardhearted man as you are!"

"Enough!" the spirit cut him short, inexorably. "You've said enough! I'm leaving. . . ."

Sinette's arms and legs twisted in atrocious convulsions. She felt as though her body were being emptied of all its substance, and her back seemed stiff and aching. And yet, moved by some secret power, she felt her body twisting into strange postures by a series of acrobatic contortions. Finally, throwing her bosom back, she held herself for a moment like an arch, her body resting only on the top of her head and her toes. Then strength slipped from her, her muscles relaxed and her body collapsed, inert, on the floor.

A heavy cloud, black as a column of smoke from a volcanic crater, poured rapidly off the mountains to the east. The cloud swiftly spread its sullen mass across the sky, collided with the sun on a level with the hilltops in the west, and hurled it beyond the range of the hills.

Daylight discreetly withdrew. Night came. The darkness was as dense as in the first days of creation, when it reigned over the blind waters of an amorphous, inanimate world, without line or color.

Then came the savage assault of the wind and rain. It passed violently over the district of Musseau, more implacable than the punishment of the gods. It flattened the flimsy houses, ripped out trees by the roots and stripped the earth. And then it engulfed them all suddenly in the numbness of complete silence. There remained only an atrocious deafness, where not even the memory of sound remained.

But soon the freshness of the earth arose from the thick Guinea grass, where it had taken refuge during the tempest. It straightened the grass again and from there it spread like a salve over the torn and bruised countryside.

Sinette left the kitchen where Desilus had dragged her, on orders from Morin Dutilleul, before she had fully regained consciousness after her fit of possession. Carrying her mat under her arm, she entered the dining room and prepared her couch for the night. She retained only a vague memory of what had happened to her that evening, just before the close of day, in the very presence of her master.

What a calling down she would get from him tomorrow morning! The poor girl trembled just thinking of it. The best thing to do, she thought, would be to leave the house for good without making a sound before Morin got up. Then, suddenly remembering the dire menace of Baron Saturday, she fell down on her knees and prayed again to the All Merciful, the miraculous Virgin of Huguey. Upstairs, despite the delicious air of peace that fell upon the earth after the storm, Morin also could not sleep. The tragic scene when Sinette had been possessed troubled him, particularly because of the strange words she had uttered in the midst of her fit.

He asked himself what this story of a candle and the werewolf could possibly mean. He had carefully questioned his hired man on the subject, but had been unable to draw anything from him which made the slightest sense. He only learned that Sinette had made a strange pact with some loa curiously named Baron Samedi, and that she had not fulfilled her obligations. As for the reasons which had led her to conclude this bargain, Desilus, while pretending not to know them, nevertheless had made some vague and confused allusions to them.

All this seemed very suspicious to Morin Dutilleul. It could only mean that the hired man was surely hatching some plot with the maid, and also without doubt, with the inhabitants of the community. Why not? They all wished him ill.

For some time now the atmosphere of this peasant setting—where the natural and the supernatural, far from being dialectically opposed to each other, were bound together into an indivisible whole—had made him extremely sensitive.

The hallucinations and nightmares which troubled his sleepless nights, and which even made him fear he might be losing his reason, surely arose from this condition. Or perhaps this might also be an effect of drink? But more than a month had passed since he had given up this vice, and he had moreover been undergoing anti-alcoholic treatments under the care of his friend, the doctor.

He came to the conclusion that his servants were feeding him one of those powerful drugs which have the terrible faculty of disintegrating a man's personality until his conscience has been completely destroyed. He knew that the secret of brewing them, which had been brought from ancestral Africa, had been handed down directly from father to son. Under these conditions, would it not be better for him to abandon his venture, sell the farm and move back to the city before it was too late?

Thus Morin reasoned with himself when the clock struck midnight.

Suddenly, before he had time to think what it could be that caused his turmoil, shivers ran up his spine, and his hair stood on end. A strange, high-pitched wailing arose from the dining room, and was prolonged in jerky vibrations.

"Hou-ou-ou-ou-ou! . . . Hou-ou-ou-ou-ou! . . ."

Sinette's voice was hardly recognizable, but he concluded that she must have been possessed again. This time the soul of some strange animal must have entered her.

He hastily lit a lamp and, having recovered from his

fright, decided to go downstairs to see what had happened to the maid.

As Morin Dutilleul came down the stairs, lighting his way with a flashlight, Sinette, whose senses were deluded, took him for an incarnation of Baron Samedi. In her delirium she even saw him wearing that spirit's picturesque clothing —his old threadbare frock coat, high opera hat, smoked glasses and the cane.

She immediately fell on her knees, opened her arms and, shaken by sobs, begged the cruel divinity to spare her.

"Mercy, Baron!" she groaned. "Mercy, I beg of you! Don't force me to fly tonight! . . . Let me repent for the wrong I have done! . . . I beg of you, father of my son! I beseech you, papa! . . . I'll do anything to make amends, but don't change me into a werewolf tonight! . . . Ai, ai! Spare me that! . . . I'll do anything you want instead!"

"But look here, Sinette!" Morin spoke as calmly as he could. "It's only me, Mister Dutilleul."

The poor girl wouldn't believe him. She only sobbed louder.

"Oh, Baron! Why should you want to fool me? I recognize you very well. You have come to transform me into a werewolf! Oh . . ."

Without further hope, she buried her face in her hands. She seemed to be suffering intensely. All the muscles of her body, agitated by convulsive shudders, moved independently of each other, in the most complete disorder.

Morin regarded her for some time and shook his head, filled with pity. Then, going near her, he touched her shoulder softly.

"What's happened to you, Sinette?" he asked.

The instant his fingers touched her, Sinette uttered a hoarse shriek, and drew back violently, as though Morin's hand had burned her flesh. Then suddenly, mimicking the flight of werewolves, with unruly bounds, she performed an unrestrained dance, her long arms flapping, frothing at the mouth and wailing.

"Hou-ou-ou-ou-ou! . . . I'm a she-devil! . . . See how well I fly, Baron! . . . Look what you've made of me! . . . Hou-ou-ou-ou-ou! Hou-ou-ou-ou-ou! . . ."

The scene was becoming fantastic. It seemed to Morin that his mind hovered on the edge of an abyss, ready to plunge into bottomless insanity. Instinctively he grabbed the maid by the waist.

"Hou-ou-ou-ou-ou! . . ." she moaned. "Why are you holding me back, Baron? Can't you see that I'm already flying?"

Morin grew impatient.

"Enough of this nonsense, Sinette!" he shouted rudely. "This joke has lasted too long already. Stop!"

She continued her violent efforts to escape from his grasp. He tightened his hold, but immediately a thrill shot through him. He could feel the ripe breasts beating against his chest, and breathed the hot peppery odor of her armpits. They brought back to him the obscure and violent pleasure she had given him one evening. Brusquely he felt the desire to taste it again.

"Furthermore," he reasoned hypocritically to himself, "it's the best way of calming her down."

And without further deliberation he threw her down on the mat, and brutally lifted her nightgown.

"Ai! Don't do that to me, Baron dear!" Sinette pleaded. "Just let me fly! I know very well that I must devour seven little infants before the break of dawn . . . Oh! Look what the Baron is doing to me! . . . Ai-ai! Leave me alone, Baron dear! Go away! Don't, please! . . ."

But all the while she begged the spirit not to violate her, Sinette avidly fluttered in the arms of Morin Dutilleul. And he felt an inexpressible voluptuousness in possessing a woman who was possessed. And what was more, he found new vigor and a juvenile pride in holding a werewolf who did him the signal honor of mistaking him for the most powerful and most formidable Baron Samedi, so that in the end it seemed to him that he truly incarnated that divinity.

Once his desire was gratified, however, he felt as though he had fallen from a great height. When he had regained his senses it was to find himself at the low ebb of sad reality described in the Ecclesiastes, and disgust almost carried the day over his vanity. Already, as in similar situations before, he recalled his dead wife.

Sinette meanwhile lay prostrate on her bed, panting but inanimate. He did not dare touch her again, for fear of arousing her. But suddenly he was seized with a fit of diabolical laughter, recalling this unbelievable, almost demoniacal, adventure through which he had just passed, in which he had played the role of a masculine demon. If he were ever to speak of it to his friends, nobody would believe him. Go tell that to others, they would say. . . .

His good humor was, alas, of short duration, for he soon heard the howling of the Cigouave. It stood right in the courtyard, making a devilish din and hurling itself against the doors of the house as if it hoped to batter them down.

Morin had had enough. Gripped by panic, he fled precipitately to the garret, where he barricaded the door and closed and bolted all the windows. Then, throwing himself upon the bed, he held his hands tightly over his ears so that he should not hear the sinister howls of the beast, nor the shrieks of Sinette. She had regained consciousness and, hearing the beast so close to her after her harrowing experience, was desperately screaming for help. . . .

esilus was seated on the doorstep of his hut, warming his aching body in the sun. His rheumatic "twinges" had returned in the night because of the heavy humidity, and he sat still, a stick between his legs, in motionless contentment, like a lizard.

Not the slightest thought disturbed the warm and torpid waters of his brain, which had slowly melted under the benign influence of the intense heat. With sad and empty eyes he peered at the countryside, still bathed in the blue morning haze.

So profound was the hired man's delight that he did not see poor Sinette approach, carrying a bundle of all her belongings wrapped in a bandana. She was hurrying away from Musseau, leaving behind forever the house of Morin Dutilleul.

"Ho-ho!" he exclaimed with a start, when she stood before him. "Ho-ho! Sinette, is that you I see before me? Are you leaving?"

"Certainly, Desilus. How could you expect me to remain here after everything that happened yesterday?"

"Don't say that, please! You're not going to walk out on us, just like that? Well!"

The maid sighed.

"If you knew what happened to me during the night, Desilus, you would not ask such a question. Do you recall Baron Samedi's threat?"

Desilus shivered, his eyes dilated with fear, and he dared not believe his ears.

"What do you mean, Sinette! Did you really fly as a werewolf last night?"

"If that was all that happened to me, Desilus, it would have been nothing. But no sooner had I been transformed into a werewolf, than Baron Samedi himself appeared before me."

"Oh-ho!" Desilus gulped. "Ho-o-o-o!"

"Wait a minute, that's not all that happened. Who do you think it was that the Baron possessed for this purpose? Mast' Dutilleul!"

"Master Morin himself?"

"Himself, in person! You never suspected that, did you? Very well, neither did I! It reminds me of an old saying I learned when I was a child: You only see the cat walking, but that's not the way she catches mice!"

"My God, Sinette! . . . So Mist' Dutilleul also serves the spirits?"

"Ai! Listen to him! But you still haven't heard everything. Baron came down from the garret, a flashlight in his hand. I asked his pardon, I begged him not to force me to fly. And what do you think he replied? That it was not the Baron, but only Mast' Dutilleul, who stood there before me!"

"Ou-o-o-oh! Sinette, you don't say!"

"It was exactly as I'm telling you, Desilus! But that's still nothing. I began to fly. I flew, I flew, I flew. And then the Baron also flew. He flew beside me and seized me in his arms. He threw me to the ground. He lifted my dress, and then—"

Tears streamed down her cheeks.

"Ai, Desilus! If I were to tell you what happened next, you would not dare believe me!"

"Enough, Sinette!" the hired man pleaded. "Peace! When the words are too strong, the jaws swell."

The maid wiped her eyes and blew her nose.

"Please, Desilus, tell me what must I do now to get out of this trouble?" she asked.

"What must you do, my daughter? I've repeated it to you since yesterday afternoon. Didn't I urge you to go at once to Rossini? If you had only listened to me, believe me, all this wouldn't have happened to you. You will say that the Baron is a man without pity, and I must admit that you are right. But there is a proverb which says: If you are inclined to blame the sparrow hawk, scold the mother hen first. And that's perfectly true. Because, if the mother hen had guarded her chicks well, the sparrow hawk would never have pounced on them."

"So then, Desilus, your advice is that I go see Rossini?"

"But, of course, my daughter. He is the one who called on the Baron to intercede for you. And so he alone can now plead for you before his judgment seat. You must go this very moment and find Rossini. He will tell you just what you will have to do. After that you should wait for me at my godmother Viergine's house, right next door. I will come and meet you there this afternoon."

"Will you really, Desilus? You won't abandon me?"

"My word is as good as gold," the hired man answered gravely.

Desilus kept his word. He rejoined the maid at his friend's house, shortly after lunch. The two women were drinking

their coffee and talking with animation. The maid had told
Viergine all, and the latter was explaining to her the dangers of abandoning the cult of the jungle gods and obeying
the commandments of the Catholic religion.

"Don't you see, daughter?" she was saying. "Even the
Protestants, about whom there is so much talk these days,
can not turn away completely without danger from the
worship of the spirits. I knew a poor woman once. Assefi
was her name. One day, just like that, I don't know what
it could have been that hit her, she joined the Adventist
Church. She rejected the loas. But three months later, what
do you think happened? A spirit entered her head and
asked the family why it was that Assefi no longer left food
for him. They told him that she had become a Protestant.

" 'Aha, so that's it!' the spirit said, in a rage. 'So she did
that without even asking my permission?'

"He had hardly finished speaking through her own
mouth, that spirit, than he threw the woman violently to
the ground. Then he took her head and bashed it against
the walls of the house. And when he left the body, Assefi
was dead, her skull crushed and all her blood streaming out
of her body like a river. . . ."

At this point in her tale Desilus limped in. Having
greeted his godmother, he excused himself and drew
Sinette to one side.

"What did Rossini say?" he asked her.

"He can fix up everything with the assistance of an
itinerant voodoo priest, who will perform an act of grace
for me. It's to be this afternoon. I think it's already time to
go."

So they went together to the houngan's house.

The altar was set up right in the middle of the thatched

hut. It was made of a little table covered by a white table-cloth, on which two bouquets of flowers and two candles had been placed, one at each corner, with the candles in front and the flowers behind. They had already served up on the table the traditional feast offered to Baron Samedi. There was the black cock, which is the Baron's symbol, fish, bananas, sweet potatoes, yams and boiled beef. Nor had they forgotten the popcorn and the grilled pistachio nuts, the candies, the sweet buns, the cassavas and the rum claret, which he dotes on more than anything else.

The itinerant voodoo priest was not late in arriving.

He was a short, squat man, broad-backed, and as unctuous as the village priests he had known when he had been sexton in the chapel at Delmas. He wore a black beard streaked with gray, trimmed and frizzled.

Rossini introduced Sinette and Desilus to him, and he gravely greeted them, ceremonious in his overstarched white suit and rigid celluloid collar. To show that he had little time to lose, he asked:

"Is everything ready?"

When Rossini assured him that they were ready he took a prayer book from his pocket. The houngan first lit the two long candles on the altar, and then the black candle of Baron Samedi which had been placed on the ground, at the entrance to the houmfor. Having completed these preparations, the itinerant preacher, after blessing himself in a tremulous and crackling voice, recited three Our Fathers, three Hail Marys, one I Confess, and the Litany of the Saints. Then he sang a hymn of his own composition, in which the Creole and French tongues were strangely intermingled.

"Mercy, Mary! Have Mercy!
Mercy, Mary! Have Mercy!
Pardon, my good Jesus!
Pardon, my good Jesus!
It's pardon that I ask of you!
Saint Philomena, martyred Virgin,
Grant us forgiveness!
"Saint Philomena, guard us well!
We bow down before thy power!"

He had not yet completed his hymn when Baron
Samedi, slipping into the body of Rossini, sang in his turn
with a nasal twang:

"Here I am! Oh! I have returned!
Baron Saturday,
Baron of the Cross,
Baron of the Cemetery!
My friends, have you ever seen
    anything like it?
An adder has crossed the threshold!"

The itinerant priest offered him a goblet filled with
water. He brusquely took it, without thanks, poured three
libations before the altar, and then seizing Sinette by the
hand, made her pirouette thrice where she stood. Then he
ordered her down on her knees to ask his pardon, which
she did in a trembling voice, shaking in every muscle.

"This time I forgive you," the Lord of the Guedes, or
nether spirits, said. "But beware that this never happens
again, for then you will find me pitiless."

Sinette, having thanked him effusively, brought him

food. He offered some to the itinerant priest as well as Desilus, who thanked him for this signal honor. It was not the Baron's habit to be generous. Having fortified himself from the dishes that had been prepared for him, and drunk deeply of the white rum, into which pimento and two-starred anise had been soaked, he turned again to the young woman.

"This time you must put on a penitent's dress and make a pilgrimage to the Chapel of the Two Hermits."

And then he withdrew.

The itinerant priest explained to Sinette that the dress of which the Baron had spoken must be made of Siamese cloth or of white calico. Moreover, she would have to wear a blue madras bound about her head and a black scarf tied about her waist while on the pilgrimage. And on that day she must offer coffee and bread to all those she found at the chapel. After the ceremony she must give the sacristan fifty centimes, and ask him to pray for her before the grotto of the Virgin of Huguey. . . .

As she was bidding him farewell, the hired man said to Sinette:

"I almost forgot to tell you about Mist' Dutilleul. You know, this morning he came to ask me where you had gone. I told him that I hadn't seen you since the evening before."

"And what did he say to that, Desilus?"

"He didn't flinch. But he seemed very strange and appeared embarrassed. He asked me: 'So she quit the job?' I answered by saying: "Ho-ho! Mist' Dutilleul! How should I know?' He bowed his head, turned red as a tomato and asked again: 'But why should she do that?' But before

I could open my mouth to answer him, he turned his back on me, and I heard him mutter to himself: 'It's very curious, for I paid her well enough!' Then he returned to the house, almost running."

Sinette was upset and tried to end the discussion. But Desilus held her back by the arm.

"I believe," he said to the maid, "that Mist' Dutilleul regrets losing you. At heart, you know, he really isn't at all bad. It's only that his blood is hot. You should return to him, now that the Baron has granted you his pardon."

"No!" exclaimed the young woman, holding back her tears with difficulty, but still firm in her resolution. "No, Desilus! I will not go back to Mast' Dutilleul's service. When I have made my pilgrimage, I am going back to my own village, to Leogane. It's been more than two years since I last saw my mother."

For an instant they looked sadly at each other. Then Desilus sighed.

"After all, Sinette," he said, squeezing her hand, "perhaps you are right. You have just come back from far, far away, you know. . . ."

Some time later, overwhelmed by a profound lassitude, Morin Dutilleul left Musseau, abandoning the farm to the sole care of his hired man. He had grown daily more disgusted with himself and this country life, which he felt he had ruined. His town house was no longer rented, so he installed himself in it again and continued his morose existence.

Every morning he would carry flowers to the cemetery. He would place them, trembling, on his wife's grave, and then walk away quickly, like a criminal fleeing the place of his crime. From time to time he found other flowers freshly left by some unknown hand upon the marble tombstone on which Eugenie's name was engraved. He was eager to know who was the person who was moved by such piety toward his dead wife. It must certainly be one of her former friends, but which one might it be? He had never been able to surprise her at the grave.

This interest aroused only moderate curiosity in him, for he expected nothing more from life. Only Saturdays brought a slight distraction in his life, when Desilus came to receive his weekly wages. He always brought something from the farm, fruit, vegetables, eggs and even chickens from time to time. Morin would then ask him for news of what was going on up there in the hills. The hired man invariably would answer that things were going along tolerably well, and he did not lie. He had brought one of his nephews to help him with his farm work.

But one day he arrived more crestfallen than before.

His limp had become worse and his whole aspect had become so pitiful that Morin kindly inquired:

"Now what's gone wrong, Desilus?"

"Oh, nothing! Nothing at all, Mist' Dutilleul."

"But I can plainly see that you are upset, even discouraged. . . . Could it be that the Cigouave has returned to make more trouble for you?"

"Oh no, Master! Ever since you came down from up there, it has never come around to bother us. And so people are asking if it had not really been sent against you . . . But this week we've had another burden dumped on our heads. Bossuet himself has returned!"

Morin started up.

"Bossuet! Do you really mean that, Desilus?"

"Yes sir! He's been back since last Sunday. And he immediately began doing things that have set all tongues wagging about him. Mist' Dutilleul, do you know that he ran off with Irma, and has set up living with her right under his own wife's nose? And she, poor woman, didn't dare say a word to him! How he managed that, nobody knows. Alcaeus tried to take his daughter back, but Sheriff Delice, who is now a damned soul completely under Bossuet's power, arrested the old man for creating a public scandal and dragged him off to prison."

"That isn't possible, Desilus! Did he really do such a thing?"

"I'm telling you, Mist' Dutilleul, so you can believe me. And that's not all. My rheumatic twinges have returned in the last three days, stronger than ever. They first came with the appearance of the Cigouave and they went away with its disappearance. But no sooner did Bossuet return to Musseau than they began to torment me once more."

"Do you think there's any connection there, Desilus?

Didn't you tell me before that it was your son who was causing you this suffering?"

"That's true enough, I admit, Mist' Dutilleul. But you don't understand. Although he's my son, he is even more Bossuet's godson, and therefore entirely under his influence. . . ."

The following Saturday the hired man looked more crushed than before.

"Mist' Dutilleul," he said, "my body is no longer good for anything. I feel that I am dying. If you do not come to my help, before long you will be obliged to look for another hired man to farm your land, for Desilus will no longer be there!"

"Well, what can I do for you, Desilus?"

"Mist' Dutilleul, for a long time now there has been a certain duty that I should perform, but I've never had the money to do it. And that's why you now see me in this sad condition. Well, I thought maybe you could help me by paying me a month's wages in advance."

"I'd like to very much, Desilus. But, tell me, what sort of duty is this that you must carry out?"

"Now, please don't get angry with me. Please! . . . Well, then. Ever since the death of my wife, and that's already more than two years ago, I haven't offered any food to my family loas, and they have become angry with me. That's why they've withdrawn their protection from me, so that my little son and Bossuet are free to inflict any harm they want on me. The week before last I went to see Rossini, the houngan of Musseau, who is a good friend of mine. He was willing at his own expense to perform a little service for me. But the spirits were unable to enter his voodoo chapel, because All-Bountiful Legba, who is incensed at me for having chopped down his votive tree, would not consent to clear the way so that they might pass. Now I must offer him a special service, to him alone, so that he will forgive that offense and let me intercede with my family gods. And I couldn't ask Rossini to do that at his own expense! That's why I have come to you to ask for an advance on my wages."

"I would like nothing better than to do such a service for you, Desilus," replied Morin. "But not so that you should squander your money on that houngan. Moreover, I'm convinced that all these notions you have in your head about your son and Bossuet are nothing but pure nonsense. Desilus, you are simply ill. I am sure that the pains you feel come from that bad case of yaws you have on your back and legs. Now what you should really do is to go to the hospital where they will take good care of you, and in a few days you'll feel much better. A little longer and you'll be completely cured. And I will foot the entire bill until you are well. But as for advancing you money to throw away on one of those superstitious ceremonies, that I will never do!"

Desilus did not argue with him. He did not insist. He simply refused the offer of treatment in the hospital. He said he couldn't go just then, but would consider it awhile first. Then he went away.

Morin Dutilleul was never to see his hired man again. Each Saturday thereafter the nephew came to collect his wages. Morin would ask him for news about Desilus, and the other would answer:

"He's not doing so badly, no sir."

But the fact was that Desilus sank lower and lower each

day. He hardly ate any more. He had to be forced to eat. He lay all the time hunched up on his mat and would not answer when spoken to. He had even gone beyond the stage of complaining any more. And his eyes, already fixed and glassy, seemed to be looking far away into the distance, far beyond the walls of his tiny thatched hut.

He dragged on like that for three weeks and then one afternoon he was seized with a fit of hiccoughs. His nephew recognized from this sign that he was in his death agony, and losing his head, he ran off, leaving the dying man by himself. He ran to the highway without knowing where he was headed. There he met the justice of the peace, who was just on his way over to get news about Desilus.

"What are you racing along like that for?" Sheriff Delice asked him.

"Uncle Desilus!" the boy stammered, panting. "Something has happened to him."

"All right, all right! Calm yourself. What is it? Is your Uncle Desilus dead?"

"Not yet, Sheriff. But he just had a violent attack of hiccoughs. If he hasn't strangled by now, I'd be surprised."

"And is that any time to run away, instead of staying there to help your old uncle? Honestly, sometimes I wonder where they stuck your head! Come along with me now. We can't let your uncle die like that, without anyone near to close his eyes, all alone like a dog!"

They found Desilus sitting upright on his mat, in an extreme state of agitation, gesticulating and shouting like a lunatic—a real vision of hell! The doomed man kept repeating one phrase endlessly between his gasps for breath:

"He must, he must, he must, he must! . . . He must, he

must, he must, he must, he must! . . . I say; he must, he must, he must, he must. . . ."

As soon as he saw him in this condition, the justice of the peace guessed what was up. Ogoun Badagris, Desilus' guardian spirit, not wishing him to die yet, had no doubt possessed him to keep a spark kindled in the old carcass.

And Delisca was not mistaken.

"What!" the spirit shouted with astonishment when he saw the two men. "Have you come here alone? But where is the inheritor of his soul?"

And as the others stood gaping, he made his meaning clear:

"I ask you, where is the son of my horse?"

"He is in Pétionville," answered the justice of the peace. "But if you are waiting for him, we will fetch him at once."

"He must, he must, he must, he must! . . ." roared the spirit. "He must, he must, he must, he must! . . ."

And he kept up this excited monologue until they finally fetched the child.

"At last! There you are!" Ogoun Badagris said to him, chuckling. "How long I have waited for you, my little one! And I needed you so very much! My horse is about to die, and you must henceforth replace him. Come close to me, so that I may mount you. Come then, my ferocious little colt! Ah! how well I am going to train you! And I want you to be more faithful to me than was your father."

As the justice of the peace pushed the reluctant child into the arms of the spirit, he was seized by fright, and screamed like a child who has been skinned.

"No!" he screamed. "No, I don't want to go near him! I don't want to! I'm scared!"

But Ogoun brutally seized hold of him, thrust his forehead against his, and immediately possessed him. And the same instant, drained of the divine substance which had prolonged his life, Desilus fell back upon his matting, his eyeballs turned up. Thus he was finally able to die.

Ogoun Badagris seemed fairly well satisfied with his new mount. But he recalled that his father still owed him an offering.

"Let the family arrange it as they will," he commanded. "But they must give me something to eat. If not, I will not answer for the child's future, and he will die like his father."

With this dire threat uttered through the boy's lips, he ominously let his presence in the child be known to all.

ne day at last he met her face to face, as he was walking around one of those immodest large mausoleums with pretensions of being a chapel. He almost bumped into her.

"You!" he exclaimed with astonishment.

She seemed no less surprised than he at the encounter, but she had the distraught air of a person caught in the act of doing something wrong. Instinctively she clutched her breast, as though to hide there the flowers she was bearing to Eugenie's grave.

"Yvonne Regis!" Morin Dutilleul exclaimed, and then he added to himself, suddenly irritated, "So she was the one!"

And yet it should not have been a surprise to him, for she had been his wife's best friend. She was one of those attractive mulatto women, with a violet mouth, a provocative bosom and a roving eye, who always warmed his blood at first sight. Morin had always been annoyed in her presence, ever since their first meeting. Perhaps it was because she acted so virtuous, and even a little cold and distant towards him, despite her outward attractions.

"So, those flowers," he stammered, "were they . . . for her?"

The young woman hesitated a moment. Then, looking him sadly in the eyes, she nodded yes. Overwhelmed by emotion, Morin babbled some vague words of thanks and tried to brush past her, but she clung to him.

"Please wait for me here," she asked in a strange voice.

"I'll be right back. Just long enough to say a short prayer over Eugenie's grave."

Morin looked after her as she went away. She had grown slightly slimmer since her divorce. It had caused quite a scandal, since her husband left her with the two children to go and live with his mistress. Morin found that the change had improved her, and that her sorrow became her better than the calm, triumphant air which she formerly used to affect in his presence.

Being essentially romantic, the idea came to him that perhaps, some day, the memory of his wife would unite them, and that they might rebuild their lives together. It would be a solution which, from every point of view, could hardly be displeasing to the dead woman.

And so, when she had rejoined him, he hastened to speak to her in his warmest and most affectionate voice.

"Yvonne, I only learned of your troubles through the newspapers. If I did not come to offer my help, it was simply because at the time I was trying to regain an interest in work. And then, it would have been impossible to see you again without thinking of my dear—"

He hastily corrected himself:

"Of *our* dear departed!"

He was about to add: "She loved you dearly, you know!" but refrained, ashamed of his hypocrisy. He recalled that those had been almost exactly the last words that the dying Eugenie had whispered to him: "I loved you . . . very much . . . you know. . . ."

As he remained silent, clearly embarrassed, Yvonne Regis came to his rescue.

"I understood, Morin. Don't think I had felt the slightest ill-feeling towards you," she said.

Then she suddenly burst out sobbing, without any apparent reason, and Morin became as deeply upset as she was.

He took her tenderly by the arm.

"Yvonne, Yvonne . . . But what is it that bothers you?"

"It's nothing, Morin, nothing . . . Please go now, I beg of you. I need to be alone."

"But how could I abandon you in the condition you are in at this moment? . . . Besides, it's entirely my fault that you are crying. It was so stupid of me to talk to you of your troubles!"

"No, Morin, no! I'm not upset for the reason you think. Not that at all!"

"But then what could it be. May I know?" he asked her gallantly. "It's because of her . . . Eugenie, isn't it?"

She raised her head, and her face was imploring him in the midst of her despair . . . Ah! How beautiful she looked to him at that moment! And how strange and fascinating were her eyes!

"Please forgive me, Morin," she said to him at last. "But I knew I had to tell you about it some day. . . . Do you know that if Eugenie is dead . . . it's partly my fault!"

"But that's impossible!" he exclaimed, disconcerted. "What ever makes you think that, Yvonne?"

"You were neglecting her towards the end, she thought you no longer loved her. . . ."

"My God!" exclaimed Morin, choking.

"She was such a child, Eugenie . . . you know. As for me, I didn't know what to say to her. And she suffered so because of it, the poor little one! So I advised her to have a baby, thinking perhaps that would succeed in holding you. But I could hardly have suspected—"

She abruptly cut short her explanation. Morin Dutilleul had collapsed on a tombstone, his face was haggard. At last he was convinced that it had indeed been himself and his loose conduct which had caused the death of his wife.

"Forgive me!" Yvonne Regis repeated to him again. She could not have understood that she had just struck him a mortal blow.

His look had become so strange that she hurried away without even looking back. She, at least, had been lightened of a heavy burden by confessing what she believed had been her own sin. . . .

Morin Dutilleul entered the little café near the cemetery. Although he had been a regular customer in the past, now for the first time he noticed the sign above the bar door: "Here you'll feel a lot better than across the street."

He shrugged his shoulders and sighed. "And they think that's funny!"

As for him, it was clear that he would never laugh again. There was nothing left but to drink as he had drunk before; to drink until he perished.

As soon as he was seated he ordered an absinthe, then another. He was bitterly satisfied to find his old thirst was as vigorous as in the days when he could stay drunk all day long. So there was nothing more to do than to satisfy that thirst.

"Moreover," he said to himself, "proverbs never lie. 'He who has drunk . . .' "

What an idiot that doctor had been, trying to make him believe that he could get rid of his vice! Anyhow, wasn't it better for him, since he had nothing more to expect from this world, that intemperance should really be incurable?

And so he reasoned, in order to fool the deep remorse he felt. In truth he had no really great desire to destroy himself. The instinct of self-preservation still bound him to this life by a thousand mysterious ties.

"The dirty slut!" he muttered to himself, thinking of the cruel admission Yvonne Regis had just made to him. "And the ironical way in which, after having injected her poison into me, she said to me, 'Forgive me!'"

To think that for an instant he had thought it possible to build a home with her! How naïve he had been to think that she had changed. She had attracted him once more, but only to play with him, as in the past . . . And then . . . No, that wasn't the way it really was! He himself was the guilty one, the traitor, the imposter, the lecher; the one who had always secretly coveted her! . . . He had done it again, just a little while ago, right beside Eugenie's grave! . . . Didn't it seem like fate? . . . "Oh, certainly!" he said to himself. "You'd just love to call that by some respectable name! Then what about Sinette? And all the others? . . . Away with you, you dirty hypocrite! . . ."

Unable to appease this torment inside him, he ordered drink after drink and was not long in passing out under the table. . . .

When he came to it was almost dark. The café owner wanted to call a cab for him, but he refused, insisting that he wanted to drink more. The owner tried to reason with him.

"You will be sick, sir, if you go on drinking. It would be much better if you were to go home now."

Morin wouldn't listen to him, and as the other persisted in his refusal to serve him any more drinks, he grew angry.

"Since you don't want to," he said thickly, "then I'll go
find a drink somewhere else. So there! Han!"

And off he went, reeling from side to side, to the great
disgust of all he met.

He lived this way for a whole week. Then, one evening,
without any idea of how he had gotten there, he woke up
at Musseau, lying in his own bed in the garret.

And the Cigouave was standing there beside the bed,
close to him, its phosphorescent eyes fixed upon him. It
was panting like a dog, with dripping jowls hanging
loosely.

In one bound Morin Dutilleul had reached the staircase.
He cleared it in three jumps, threw open the door and
dashed off into the night. But the Cigouave pursued him
without flagging.

At certain moments, when fatigue made him slow down
his mad pace, he would feel the burning breath of the
beast upon his neck. Then he would redouble his speed. It
became a terrifying chase, frantic, silent, for the monster
did not howl and no sound could issue from the throat of
Morin Dutilleul.

Without knowing it, he finally reached the Petionville
highway, rushed straight ahead, ran against the guard-rail
and tumbled into the ravine.

To tell how Pierre and I wrote *The Beast of the Haitian Hills*, as well as our two other novels, I have to go back to an earlier time, and I must acknowledge my debt to a United States writer, who, although he died many years ago, is still anathema to my countrymen. For it all began in 1932 with *The Magic Island*, which I had just read in the French translation and in which William Seabrook, while painting a sensational and fanciful picture of the ruling class of Haiti, based on gossip and snap judgments, nevertheless presented the peasantry of the country and its religious beliefs in a human and sympathetic light.

Until then, like all the people of the bourgeois milieu to which I belonged, I considered the *Vodoun* cult a body of superstitious practices, grotesque as well as dangerous, probably including human sacrifice and even ritual cannibalism. To be sure, contemporary Haitian authors had written about the popular religion of the country from a sociological and even a medical point of view, and had denied all the legends which linked it with witchcraft. But it was Seabrook's work which changed my attitude by revealing to me that the *Vodoun* cult constituted a rich mine of material in which humor and fantasy blended with pathos and poetry, and by showing me the excellent use I could make of it in the literary field.

It was at this point that I felt compelled to "go down" among the people, in order to see their life close up, to learn their language and to find out their way of thinking. It was anything but easy, because until then my only contact with them had been through our servants, who certainly had taken me into the enchanted world of our folk tales but had not allowed me to glimpse either their inner life or religious beliefs. In the beginning, if I ventured alone into a *Vodoun* ceremony, I was admitted with distrust if not outright hostility; but in the course of time, thanks to several acquaintances of mine from the lower middle class—who secretly worshiped the African gods—I succeeded in being accepted on an equal footing. Thus in less than three years, to the great shock of my family and friends, I became intimate with several sanctuaries of this disparaged cult.

I first applied myself to unraveling the complexity of the ritual and mythology; I collected the hymns and recorded the proverbs and formulas which constitute the foundation of these songs and facilitate the improvisation of new ones. It was fascinating work for the born researcher, but quite intoxicating. The fact is that I was almost literally spellbound, to the point that I no longer frequented my club and almost deserted my home.

However, I did not progress in the direction I had charted for myself. Instead of using the material whose richness Seabrook had shown me, I continued writing poems, literary and political articles, and short stories more or less based on bourgeois life. The reason was very simple. I had "gone down" among the people, but I saw them only from the outside and took no part in their everyday life. I took no steps to be initiated into the mysteries of their religion; I never ate their food except when a refusal might be discourteous. In other words, the people were for me just an object for study, and despite a constantly growing sympathy for them, my approach was little different from a foreign ethnologist's. Besides, while I expressed myself in Creole, my language was to a great extent Gallicized, and it sometimes happened that my informants and I did not completely understand each other.

I should probably never have got out of this impasse if my brother Pierre, to whom I had confided my doubts on the matter, had not finally proposed that we collaborate in writing a novel based on peasant life. Until then he had scarcely shown a penchant for a literary career, except that he had written one short story. My first reaction was therefore to reject his proposal: since he was not a professional writer, how could he help solve the problems which seemed insoluble to me, the most important of which was to put the myths into action as Homer and the Greek writers of tragedy had done? Then I recalled that he had lived for some time in the country and had even been involved in an agricultural enterprise. Moreover, since his childhood he had always been recalcitrant toward bourgeois life, rather seeking out the company of the humble, whose friendship he won because of his modesty and natural kindness. He had thus acquired a broad knowledge of their language and their way of thinking, and therefore he could contribute all I lacked. So I did not long hesitate in accepting the collaboration he wholeheartedly offered me.

First we agreed on the general plan he submitted. Then we decided that, after our discussion of each chapter, he would write the first draft in which the characters would speak in Creole and I would be responsible for the final writing. This is the way we have worked, and we hope to continue the same way if we have the good fortune of being together in Haiti for at least a year—which has not been possible since 1948, when political circumstances forced me to live outside my country.

The first collaboration was difficult, although Pierre showed from the beginning, and to my great surprise, a comprehensive knowledge of the technique of the novel. His indifference to style, for which he left me the entire responsibility, was disconcerting. Nor did I share his assurance that we would find a publisher in the United States—hence my decision, to which he reluctantly agreed, that in the final text our characters would speak in Creole. Besides, the rural community where the action takes place was fast becoming a suburb of Port-au-Prince; ruined by the limekilns which proliferated with the building boom, the landscape had lost all the grace of this idyllic countryside where our family used to have a summer home, and as I had not spent the holidays there since I was nine years old, I had to depend entirely on my childhood memories for the descriptions which were also my responsibility.

Our disagreements on all these points were such that, by 1942, our novel—which we finally entitled *Canapé-Vert*, after the name of a hill neighboring our property in Bourdon—had already been reworked four times. It was at that point that the Second Latin American Literary Contest (organized by Farrar and Rinehart under the auspices of the Pan American Union) was announced. And for my penance, though I was still far from sharing Pierre's optimism, I was obliged to translate the dialogues and songs into French before we could enter our novel in the contest.

One can imagine my astonishment and joy when I heard on Pan American Day, April 14, 1943, the official announcement that out of 20 competitors from the Hemisphere, we had won the prize for the novel (an advance of

$2,000 against royalties—a fabulous sum for Haitian writers who had never been published except at their own expense, and usually in editions of fewer than 500 copies). All the educated people, and even the illiterate ones who heard the news on the radio, were elated over our success, which was considered something of a national triumph. The Senate voted us congratulations, and the President of the Republic, who was inclined like so many Haitian heads of state to consider himself the Lord's Anointed, invited me to a private audience. It was even suggested that we be decorated with the order "Honneur et Mérite," a distinction to which we did not in the least aspire (and which in the end we did not receive).

The honeymoon was soon over. The natural envy of our brother-writers was revealed immediately after the publication of the book in New York and the translation in Haiti of the favorable reviews which appeared in the United States press. They found their pretext in a fact for which we were in no way responsible: the translator, who interpreted our text quite freely, presented *Canapé-Vert* in a preface which, though well meant, was full of inaccuracies. And it could not but wound the ultrasensitive Haitian feelings.

However, our great sin was that we had presented the life of peasants at grips with poverty and religious taboos, instead of idealizing them or vindicating the upper class. The reproach was not made openly but by insidious gossip. The result was that after several months, though I had been a civil servant for over 13 years (first as Budget Officer, then as Executive Secretary in the Department of Public Works), my job was "abolished" during the course of an administrative reorganization. Subsequently the President of the Republic, rebuked by a mutual friend for my dismissal, simply replied, "I wouldn't bother about him."

It was in this depressing climate that my brother and I wrote *The Beast of the Haitian Hills*. The idea for it came to us when we were working on the first draft of *Canapé-Vert*, but at that time we envisaged it in the form of a satiric work depicting a community in the grip of a collective mythomania. At that time, the rural community of Musseau, where one of our uncles had a farm, was said to be haunted by a fantastic beast which the peasants called the Cigouave. Pierre often visited our relative, who was, like him, an irresistible storyteller, and he would come back with reports of the monster's imaginary exploits. As a matter of fact, "the beast" was merely terrifying the inhabitants of the region and engaging in the nocturnal theft of a chicken here, a goat or a pig there. Since our uncle was not subject to hallucinations, he had never seen the Cigouave, and he wisely concluded that the rumors were started by clever pilferers so they could steal in perfect safety.

But we later discarded the idea of treating the subject in a grotesque way. As we worked out the plan of the novel, we decided to oppose a bourgeois atheist to a well-to-do peasant who knew how to read and write but was addicted to the practices of black magic. Then we realized that the work would gain in intensity if we gave it a tragic turn. To this end, it became necessary that the character from the city, despite his sophistication and basic skepticism, should finally be taken in by the irrational ambience in which he was living and that he should eventually "see" the Cigouave. This is why we made the character an alcoholic and a widower tormented by the suspicion that he had indirectly caused the death of his wife; the Beast finally embodies his guilt.

Our collaboration was easier this time; we started writing the novel about April 1944 and finished it in May of the following year. The English translation, published in New York in 1946, met with the same reception as had *Canapé-Vert*. But, dreading the reaction of our countrymen, we restrained the impulse to publish the American reviews in Haiti. This would doubtless have rekindled their patriotic wrath, for the grievousness of our sin lay in the fact that we were translated and published abroad.

Having bought our peace at this price—high indeed for our authors' vanity—we were able to write in less than six months *The Pencil of God*, whose main theme is calumny. Of course, the subject of the novel is derived from our own experience. And if we treated it with humor, blending the grotesque with the tragic, it was by way of exorcism in order to free ourselves of the demon of bitterness.

—Philippe Thoby-Marcelin